Were Chronicles

PACK HUNTER

CRISSY SMITH

Pack Hunter
ISBN # 978-1-78686-348-5
©Copyright Crissy Smith 2018
Cover Art by Posh Gosh ©Copyright March 2018
Interior text design by Claire Siemaszkiewicz
Totally Bound Publishing

Totally Bound Publishing books by Crissy Smith

Were Chronicles
Pack Alpha
Pack Enforcer
Pack Territory
Pack Rogue
Pack Community
Pack Mates
Pack Daughter
Pack Hunter

Shifter Chronicles
Birds of Prey
Bear Claw
Eye of the Tiger
Coyote's Kiss
Wolf Pack
Lion's Claim

Bloodlines
Bite
Control
Embrace

What's Her Secret?
Designated Alpha

PACK HUNTER

Dedication

For my sister, my rock, a true friend.

Chapter One

Clint Price jogged down the large gravel drive on his way to the guardhouse. The morning sun had already started to bathe the beautiful property in its colorful rays. The property he was staying on was magnificent. Clint enjoyed the lush green lawns and wide-open space. The dense forest called out to him, but it wasn't time for *that* kind of run yet.

Two guards, Alan and Jody, saw him heading in their direction and opened the side fence so he didn't have to slow down. He waved in appreciation as he passed, and they laughed, waving back. They were used to his morning routine by now.

It had been over a month since he'd first arrived at the Alpha Council compound in northern California. The group of guys he worked with daily had become great friends. Clint didn't know how much longer he and his best friend, Kurt Moore, would be staying. They often took jobs in different Packs to help with security. Their years of serving in the military and getting the best training available ensured they had plenty to offer shifters. He enjoyed what he did, for the most part.

Clint had been traveling for so long that when he had to stay in one place, he grew agitated. Kurt was his family, and that was all he needed. Or it had been. This stop in California had actually opened his eyes to another need he thought he'd buried deep. Clint had never wished to settle down. Not in a town or with one woman. But maybe things were changing. He blew out a long, deep breath and picked up his pace.

From the entrance of the compound, he started south toward the town of Lovington, the huge property now at his back.

He never missed his run. Not only did it help keep him in shape, but the freedom of running also kept him from going stir crazy. Every morning, he ran in his human form, and every evening he shifted and ran as his wolf.

The Alpha compound was one of the nicest he had ever been on. Hidden in the northern mountains of California, the compound housed eight wolf Alphas, who served as the Council for the Packs of the United States. While the actual location of the Council compound was only known by a handful of people, the property stayed on constant high alert to keep the Council members safe at all times.

The shifters of the world had revealed their existence not too long ago. While the majority of humans had been shocked, most had taken to the shifters without problems.

But, as with anything, there were some who couldn't accept the differences in the shifters and had named them evil and threatened them.

Four weeks ago, a Pack close to the Alpha compound had been almost devastated by fires around their community. Five fires in total, but luckily no one had been injured or killed. The Pack had fought back. Kurt, a member of the Pack, and Clint, along with two of their buddies, had gone there to help. With the assistance of the Pack members, they had been able to capture and arrest eight humans and two shifters. Clint and Kurt had escorted the two shifters to the compound for interviewing. Clint hadn't been involved further, but he knew Kurt remained immersed in the investigation.

Meanwhile, Clint had been asked to remain there as a guard while the Council members tried to find out what threats still remained. He had also been asked to think about accepting a permanent role as head guard. Clint was considering the job offer, but his decision would also depend on Kurt. They'd been friends since they'd first met on the Marine Corps boot camp bus heading to Parris Island.

Theirs was a friendship made through tough circumstances and loyalty. They'd been stationed together several times before both had been recruited into the Special Forces.

At the time, the government hadn't known about shifters. Having one of his kind by his side had made it easier for Clint to get through the last ten years.

They'd been through so much together. He considered Kurt his brother.

Kurt knew of Clint's interest in a local, but since Clint hadn't made a move, he couldn't base his decision to stay on one woman. Even if he wanted to. What kind of idiot decided his future on the basis of what *might* happen with another person? Clint was close to being that idiot.

It was so unlike him that Clint was at a standstill on what to do about anything related to his future.

His footsteps echoed along the empty road as he hit his stride and relaxed into the routine of his run. He let his mind clear and just concentrated on breathing.

Before he knew it, he'd reached the edge of town. Lovington was a small community, and while they now knew about shifters, they had no idea what a powerful group lived miles up the road. To the outside world, the Council pretended to be just another Pack. They were in no way a normal wolf Pack, though. Those in position ruled the wolf shifter world as a Council. Other Alphas didn't even know where the Council was located.

Packs contacted the Council by phone and email and only the highest-ranking Alphas had the opportunity to travel to the compound. Clint worked directly for the Council, but even he'd had to work for them for several years before he knew the Council location.

Once he reached town, he slowed, coming to the post office. He started his stretches and waved at Mrs. Carson as she passed on her way to the flower shop she owned. The older woman beamed at him, returning his wave. Relaxed and loose, he made his way into the post office and checked his box. There were only three items. A bill, a magazine and a letter. He looked at the return address and snorted. His buddy Samson wrote him every month. The letter could contain information about Samson's job or his family, but most of the time he sent jokes or raunchy articles. Samson refused to get with the times and use social media or email. Samson claimed he was old-school. Clint believed his friend was merely stubborn. Clint loved that about Samson.

Samson was a character—however, he was also a dependable friend who Clint was glad he'd met in the military.

Samson was human, but Clint didn't hold that against him. He was still a badass.

Clint tucked his mail under his arm before giving the man behind the counter a smile. Then he headed back out to the street.

His next stop was his favorite. If Clint were being honest with himself, the reason why he ran toward town instead of taking the route around the compound was because of his next stop.

The Blend and Brew Coffee House was located right in the middle of town in one of the storefronts on Main Street. He and Kurt had found the coffee shop their first week there. The atmosphere was homey and comfortable, the coffee perfectly blended, but it was the service that had him going back every morning.

He pulled open the door, breathing in the intoxicating aroma of freshly ground coffee, absorbing the hum of the espresso machine and laughter from the patrons.

He grinned at the sight of the woman behind the counter.

Today, she had her light-brown hair pulled back in a ponytail away from her face. Her hazel eyes sparkled as she joked with the college-aged kid working alongside her while she dumped espresso shots into paper cups.

She was several inches shorter than Clint's six-foot-one frame. Just the right size, in his opinion. She wore her usual uniform of jeans and T-shirt under her brown apron with a picture of three coffee beans dancing on the front. It was cute, yes, cute. Clint snorted. He'd never found anything cute until he'd met Sara. She was messing with everything that he'd ever known about himself.

A natural hunter, Clint knew he could come across as dangerous. Hell, he *was* dangerous. But Sara made him

Crissy Smith

feel like he could be a better person. That he had more to offer. It was a strange sensation that crawled down his spine each time he set eyes on her.

As Clint stepped toward the counter, Sara he threw her head back and laughed loudly. Clint's cock woke up behind his running pants. Fuck, he wasn't going to be able to hide an erection. He clenched his fists, pulling up all his control. He didn't want to scare her. Sara was one of the few people who didn't make Clint feel like a monster, and he liked it that way. She was a brave woman to be able to look him in the eye, morning after morning, and smile.

He knew very little about her except that every time he woke up, she was who he wanted to see. He enjoyed the sight of her ass in her tight jeans but had to imagine what she'd look like bared and sprawled out for him.

She looked up and spied him by the door. She smiled wide and called out to him.

"Hey, Clint!"

"Sara." He sent her his best smile.

Sara Webb did her best not to let her hands shake as she spotted the man standing by the front door. Every morning like clockwork, Clint Price walked into her shop and she had to suppress the urge to leap over the counter and jump him.

A silly reaction for a grown woman, but damn, he was fine.

Clint had been coming in every day for weeks now and she still didn't know much more about him than his name. Sometimes, he had a friend with him, but she liked when he was alone. Since he was on his own today, she took the opportunity to stare at him without having to avoid his friend's knowing gaze.

Clint strolled up to the counter and she tried her best not to drool, watching his hard muscles as he walked forward. His sun-bleached blond hair, dark chocolate eyes and easy smile were always a welcome sight.

She finished the two drinks she was working on and placed them on the counter, calling for Christina to come pick up her order. Then she turned back to him while grabbing a towel to wipe her hands.

"You want your usual or do you want to be daring and try something new?" she asked like she did every morning.

He chuckled and shook his head. "The usual, please."

She waved a finger at him. "One of these days, I'll get you," she teased.

His eyes darkened and her breath caught. Damn, that flash of arousal on his face made her ache. She leaned toward him. If Clint was as interested in her, Sara didn't understand what he was waiting for. He barely flirted and never asked her out. Sara wished she had the nerve to make a move on him, but while she considered herself a progressive woman, she hadn't been able to face rejection. Maybe there was a reason Clint merely watched her with his dark eyes. He could have a wife or girlfriend back at home. Hell, who knew what went on at that big mansion up the road.

His face blanked and the spell was broken. Damn it, another missed opportunity.

Hoping to hide her blush, she turned, grabbed a large cup then filled it with the day's fresh house-blend coffee. Sara was proud of the product she was able to offer. She might own a coffee shop in a small California town, but her coffee was legendary. Even celebrities stopped in when they were close. The reputation of her coffee buyer helped draw in a crowd. Sara finished pouring, then placed the lid on before passing it over the counter to him.

"One large house blend, no sugar, no cream."

He placed three dollars on the counter and pushed the money toward her before he winked and picked up the cup. He lifted it to his mouth and drank deep. Sara was caught up watching his throat work but had to turn away when she almost moaned out loud. Wow, Sara was going to have to figure out what to do about Clint eventually.

Her barista, Cecil, caught her eye and smirked at her. She glared, but couldn't put any heat behind it. It wasn't his fault that every time Clint came into the shop she wanted to lock the doors and have him bend her over the counter.

She flushed and waved a hand over her face. It was hot in the shop today.

Clint grunted and drew her attention back to him.

"I swear the coffee gets better every day," he praised.

Too aroused to think straight, she couldn't have come back with a witty comment if her life depended on it.

He patted the counter before turning and carrying his coffee to a table by the window. He dropped what looked like mail onto the table top and took his seat.

His back was to her now. He stretched his long legs out under the table and Sara had to grip the counter to stop from offering to drop between those powerful thighs.

Cecil came up beside her and hip-checked her. "You keep staring at him like that, and we're all likely to catch on fire," he teased in a low tone.

She smacked his arm and moved away to clean up a little, taking advantage of the lack of customers. Cecil had gone back over to wipe down the espresso machine, so Sara began clearing used cups and pastry wrappers from empty tables.

As she glanced around, she saw that in addition to Clint, there were two women giggling at one table, a group of five college kids in the couch and chairs and two business men in suits.

Business was good, and for that she was thankful.

It had been a big risk opening her own business, but she had saved her money, knowing what she wanted. She had a love for coffee and books. A perfect day for her would be to curl up in a comfortable chair with a hot cup of rich coffee and the newest mystery book. She was a book geek, enjoyed her quiet, small-town life and never wanted for more. That was, until a handsome stranger had first stopped in for his morning cup.

Now, she often fantasized about more.

Not that she wanted her life to change. She was happy, but meeting Clint had reminded her of an element she hadn't realized she was missing.

She'd had plenty of relationships in the past, even a semi-serious one while attending college, but no attraction had ever been as strong as the one that drew her to Clint.

Remaining far enough from him where she could admire him without the threat of being discovered, she continued to watch him. He'd arrived in town a short time ago with Kurt. The town gossip had placed him at the shifter compound several miles up the road, so she had to assume he was one of the shifters. She didn't know much about what that meant, though.

She'd grown up in the tiny town, not knowing anything about the shifters who lived among them. Her dad still worked as the sheriff. Her mom, before she'd passed, had volunteered at the local library.

When the news about shifters being real and not mythical creatures had come out, it was only then the town had learned that the large property close by was not only owned by a rich family, but actually housed a small group of shifters. She wasn't even sure what type of animals. She'd read some news stories and several articles, but since the residents of the big house outside town had rarely visited, no one knew much about the local group.

It was only recent that the shifters had begun to appear in town regularly. Most of the younger ones, like Clint, stopped by the coffeehouse, went shopping and even grabbed a bite to eat at one of the restaurants on occasion.

Unless someone knew what they were, no one would never guess they were different.

Her dad had come clean with her after the shifters went public. He had known and had been committed to keeping the shifter existence quiet.

When she'd asked why he'd agreed to keep their secret, he'd explained to her that having the shifters there meant they would always have protection. Plus, he had informed her, it had always been that way. Even back when her great-grandfather had settled in town, the shifters had already been there. The humans had moved in and a truce had been reached.

The humans brought in businesses that were much needed to make the town look normal, while the shifters in Lovington vowed to protect everyone, shifter and human.

She could understand the logic, and it didn't make much of a difference to her. She was intrigued, but until she'd met Clint, she had never given shifters much thought.

Movement drew her eye back to the man she had been thinking about. Clint turned and tilted his head to her with a frown on his face.

She hoped that he hadn't been bothered by her attention. He had never seemed to mind before.

He didn't look back at her as he rose, then pulled open the door and disappeared onto the street. The two men in business suits from the table next to him scrambled up and quickly followed after him. She called out a farewell to them, but they didn't even acknowledge her. Clint's abrupt departure bothered her more than it should have. Usually he smiled or waved when he left.

Sara scurried back around the counter where Cecil was almost done with cleaning. She glanced at her watch and saw it was almost time to start on the books. She enjoyed working the counter for the morning rush, talking with her regulars and hearing the latest gossip. But once it started to slow down, Cecil could handle the rest of the shift.

"I'm going into the office," she told her employee.

Cecil nodded. "Don't worry about me," he told her. "I've got this."

She smiled and headed into the back where her office was located, the blond-haired, brown-eyed man still foremost in her thoughts. Sara wondered if Clint had any idea how much she craved his touch. Really, if he was a shifter wouldn't he be able to pick up on that? In one article or another, she'd read that strong shifters picked up emotions from others.

If Clint could, then maybe he was humoring her.

Sara obviously wanted him and maybe he just didn't care.

Clint continued down First Street, keeping his senses open. He pretended to window shop before he pulled his cell phone out of his pocket and pressed the speed dial number for Kurt.

His friend picked up on the second ring. "Don't tell me, you've finally decided to stay in town and take that pretty coffee shop owner up on her unspoken offer to go into the back office," Kurt said, laughing.

Clint growled. Kurt had been giving him a hard time about his daily visits to the coffee shop, asking why Clint didn't skip the coffee and take the woman. If only things were as simple as that.

"I'm being followed," Clint told him instead.

"What? Where?" Kurt became serious.

"There were two men at the coffee shop. Blue business suits. They didn't say one word to one another the entire time I was inside. But they had their eye on me, trying not to be obvious about it," Clint explained.

"Which only made it more obvious?" Kurt guessed.

"Yeah," Clint confirmed. "As soon as I left, they followed, although they're still keeping a pretty good distance."

"I'm already on my way," Kurt told him. "Try to act like you haven't seen them."

"No problem," Clint responded. He stopped in front of the candle shop and leaned closer as if he was looking at the display.

In the reflection, he could still see the two men across the street watching.

"Where are you?" Kurt asked and Clint could hear Kurt's tire squeal over the line.

"Still on First Street," Clint answered.

"Good. Head down to the park. It should be almost empty this early. I'll be there shortly. Don't kill anyone."

Clint snorted and pocketed his phone before slowly strolling to the park at the end of the block. It wasn't as though he went around and killed people. *Well, people who didn't deserve it,* he amended. And he couldn't cause trouble in the middle of town, anyway.

Clint liked the area. Loved the park.

He'd always felt comfortable coming into town. His dad had spent years working with the Alpha Council while Clint was young. His mom, brother and Clint had officially stayed in their birth Pack, but visited often. He didn't know how his parents managed such a strong marriage with his dad being away so much, but his mom and dad were happily married and still very much in love, from what he could tell.

The small park was open to the public but was mainly used for festivals. It did have a well-kept playground, several benches to sit on and even a large open space where some of the residents played football, Frisbee and other games.

He sat on one of the benches close to the street. The two men had fallen back even more, but they were still within sight. Clint stretched his legs out and massaged his calf, acting like it was bothering him.

The two men came closer and he prepared himself.

They were speaking in low tones, and Clint cursed that he couldn't make out the words. Kurt would probably have been able to. Clint's expertise was in hunting down prey, human or animal. With his military training, Clint had been able to track for miles and miles. It was said no one else in the States had the ability like him.

He waited until they were a few feet away before standing and facing them. "Can I help you gentlemen?" Clint asked in his most menacing tone.

They jerked back but didn't say anything.

"You've been following me for some time," Clint said. "What can I do for you?"

The younger one, with black hair and a sneer on his face, straightened his shoulders. "Are we supposed to be afraid of you, evil creature?" he replied, turning up his lip.

Clint leaped over the bench and grasped him by the throat, lifting him off the ground. The man struggled in his hold. His partner took a step toward Clint, but Clint just growled. He froze and Clint heard Kurt's truck skid to a stop.

His friend was beside him in seconds. "What seems to be the problem here?"

Clint shook the guy he still had a hold of. "We're evil creatures," he shared with Kurt.

Kurt shrugged. "Okay?"

The older man sputtered, "You…you p-put him down right now."

Clint scoffed, "I don't think so."

"Talk and talk fast before my friend here loses his temper," Kurt ordered.

"We only want a meeting!" he cried.

Clint lowered the younger guy but didn't release his hold. "So you insult me?"

The man shook his head. "No, no…he didn't mean it."

Clint snorted and glanced at Kurt. Kurt crossed his massive arms over his chest. "Meeting with who?"

"Your boss. We have an associate who would like to have a word with the Alpha," he said, still clearly upset.

Clint and Kurt exchanged glances. There was no Alpha there. That was not how the Council worked. So, at least these two men didn't know about the Council. That was a relief.

"And how do you know one of us isn't the Alpha?" Kurt asked with a smirk.

"The Alpha never leaves. No one has ever seen him. You two have been around town and only in the last month," the man replied smugly.

Kurt narrowed his eyes. It was obvious they had been under surveillance. "We'll pass along the message," Kurt stated.

"No, that's not good enough," the man argued. "We must present this to your Alpha ourselves. We demand you take us to him."

Clint snorted. "You have no idea who the Alpha is, and you think we'll just take you to meet him? Either you two are the biggest dumbasses I've ever met or you think we are." He lifted the man higher, then launched him several feet, making sure both strangers understood how strong they were.

The young man flew into the street, where he landed hard. He groaned and rolled into a ball.

"Your card?" Kurt asked, holding out his hand.

The older man scrambled to pull out his wallet and slapped a card into Kurt's hand, then hurried over to his partner.

Kurt motioned his head to his truck and he and Kurt climbed inside. Clint kept his eye on the side mirror until Kurt had driven them out of sight. There was no point in not going back to the compound. The location was secret, not in town anyway, but the guards were going to have to keep an eye out. While this was the reason he and Kurt were there, Clint hoped they wouldn't be trouble. Not when he was getting the nerve to settle down there.

"Man, that was fun." He sat back in his seat and grinned at Kurt.

Kurt chuckled. "I'm glad you enjoyed it. If you don't get to choke someone every few weeks, you seem to get cranky."

Clint flipped his friend off but was still smiling. "So, what was that about?"

Kurt shook his head. "They had to know that we would never have taken them into the compound. Maybe it was their way to let us know we're being watched?"

Clint chewed on his bottom lip. They had tracked him down at the coffee shop. That meant they knew his schedule. He didn't like that one bit. He didn't want to put Sara in any danger.

That thought worried him above all else.

"So how'd it go with your girl? Did you actually talk to her this time or did you grunt at her like you normally do?" Kurt asked, eyeing him with amusement.

Clint slumped in his seat. "I don't grunt at her," he argued.

"Sure, man, you don't grunt at her." Kurt laughed.

Clint ignored his friend. He was pretty sure that Sara didn't think he just grunted at her. The two strangers' eyes weren't the only ones that had been on him. While Sara had been cleaning, she had also been checking Clint out. Of course, that didn't cause the same unsettled and aggressive feelings the two men had. No, when Sara watched him, it was different. His cock perked up and his blood pumped in his veins.

For ten years, he had followed every order and given every second of his time to protect what he believed in. Now, as he moved out of that responsibility to another phase in his life, he wanted someone to share it with.

He didn't know if Sara was the one he was meant to settle down with, but she sure was who he wanted. But he couldn't exactly say that to Kurt.

Kurt had given up his first love, had only recently seen her again, and he'd had to watch her with another man.

Clint didn't believe that Kurt still loved Becca. He thought it was more that Kurt had gotten to the point where he was looking back on his life and seeing his mistakes.

They reached the gates and the same two guards as earlier waved them through.

Kurt stopped the truck in front of them. "We ran across some trouble in town. Make sure you keep an eye out. No one gets through without one of the Council's approval."

Both men nodded. "Yes, sir."

Clint grinned at the eagerness of the two guards. They had been scared shitless of Kurt and Clint when they'd first arrived. Now, it had turned to awe.

"Stuff it. They're just kids," Kurt grumbled as he drove toward the house.

"Yes, sir," Clint said as serious as he could.

Kurt ignored his cheekiness. "I'm going to take this card to the Council. You wanna come?"

Clint trusted the guards, but he wanted to check out the property himself. Plus shifting would help calm him after the spike of adrenaline from the encounter with the two humans. Clint thought it important to allow his wolf side the freedom to roam.

Being a shifter made him different from humans, but he was also considered strange by other shifters. Some shifters thought of their animal as another half. They referred to their shifter form as he or she. Clint knew the wolf was a part of him. He had the ability to transform into an incredible animal. But it was still his feelings that rushed through him even when he was covered in fur and on four feet. It was his thoughts racing as the wind ruffled his hair while he leaped and jumped. Clint was his wolf and his wolf was him.

"I think I'll check around the property. Make sure everything is secure," Clint replied. "Don't want those assholes from earlier thinking they can sniff around."

Kurt pulled the truck up to the compound and stopped. "Sounds good. I'll let them know you'll be available if they have any more questions."

They went their separate ways outside the vehicle. Kurt headed into the house and Clint continued on around the side of the building. He jogged toward the line of trees and, once under cover, started to strip. Unlike in the movies, clothes didn't shift with them or magically disappear. If they were to change while dressed, their clothes would rip and tear. Clint had lost many pairs of jeans through not being able to get naked fast enough.

He knew the rotation of the guards and had timed it so no one would come up on him in the middle of his shift. Trust was hard for Clint and transforming left him vulnerable for a few minutes.

He breathed, double-checking he was, in fact, alone. Satisfied, he dropped down and begun to shift. Luckily, his change was painless. He'd heard stories that if someone fought the change or waited too long, it could hurt.

In wolf form, he was huge. Kurt had taken a picture of him once and Clint had been impressed with his animal form. Damn, he loved to shift. The freedom of being able to do so anytime he was on the compound was one of the reasons he was thinking of accepting the Council's job offer.

Once he was on all four furry paws, he took off to run the length of the fence that surrounded the property. He trained his attention on the scents around him, making sure no one and nothing had come over the barrier and only those who belonged were present. He also kept an eye out for any weakness in the fence.

He was proud that the security was still holding strong. The compound was secure. Once he was certain everything was in place, he trotted back under cover. Instead of shifting back right away, he decided to lie under the shade of one of the trees to rest.

The events of the morning hadn't been too bad. He'd handled worse. But the possibility that he could be putting Sara and the coffee shop in danger bugged him.

It pissed him off, as matter of fact.

He would shift later and sneak back into town. He knew that Kurt would go with him if he asked, but this was something he wanted to do on his own.

Kurt would understand. His friend had been pushing Clint to make his move on Sara for a while now. Clint had been waiting until he'd made a decision whether to stay before he approached her for anything more than coffee.

The strangers in town had taken time away from his plan. But he knew he could protect Sara. Watch over the entire town if he needed to. It was what he was trained for.

He was the hunter of the unit. His senses were the sharpest of them all, and the unit he'd been assigned to had never been ambushed in all their years of service. He had experience blending in with his surroundings and knew he could get to town and back without anyone seeing him.

Resting his head on his paws, he closed his eyes and let the sounds of the leaves in the breeze sing him to sleep. In his mind, he pictured how beautiful Sara had looked that morning.

Chapter Two

Sara closed the door of the dishwasher with her hip, then remained leaning against it. She gazed out of the kitchen window that overlooked her backyard. Her night ended as most people her age were beginning theirs.

Having to get up at four every morning and be at the coffee house by five, she almost never stayed up past nine-thirty or ten.

She poured a half glass of white wine before she walked to the back door. It was dark out, but the light from her porch illuminated her garden and flowers. Her backyard was one of her favorite projects. All her extra money went to having an oasis to relax in day or night. She had several wicker chairs and couches that were perfect to snuggle in and read on the big wood deck. She even had a couple of wood benches close to her planters. Her mom's touches were everywhere back there. That was where she felt closest to the woman who'd left her too early in life.

This late in the evening, she enjoyed sitting outside and just relaxing. Nothing to do and no one she had to talk to. Her favorite time of day.

The cool night air felt like a caress as she stepped out of the back door. The last days of fall were approaching and soon winter frost would cover her yard.

Since it was such a nice night, she moved to the bench at the edge of the property. There was a small opening that led to a trail she liked to hike on her days off. She had a perfect view of the snow-covered mountains during the day, but even though she couldn't see them clearly then, she didn't mind. She'd stared at the view so many times that she could paint it with her eyes closed. That was, if she could paint at all.

She tucked her legs under her and brought the wineglass up to her lips. Another soft breeze blew over her and she shivered a little even in her pajama pants and long-sleeve Henley.

She heard a rustling sound by the trail and bent forward. Her eyes had adjusted to the low light, but she couldn't make out the shape. She squinted to see if there was any movement.

Yes, something was there.

She straightened but kept her eye on the spot where she could see the shadowed figure. It was some sort of animal, a dog or something. Yes, something that she'd spotted a couple times before. This time, she wasn't going to allow the creature the opportunity to get away from her.

She grinned. "I know you're there, and you know that I know. Why don't you come out of hiding?" she called. She didn't feel stupid talking to an animal. It wasn't like anyone else could hear her.

She almost dropped her wineglass when the animal started crawling forward. As soon as she got a good look, she knew it wasn't a dog. It was a wolf! And the size of it. Wow!

The wolf stopped.

"Oh, no, baby, don't stop now," she murmured.

She should be out of her mind with fear, but she was so excited. She hadn't seen anything so gorgeous in her life.

The wolf crept forward. Pure white — not a spot of another color that she could see. She sat her wineglass on the ground next to her and gripped her knees to keep from reaching out to the animal.

Her fingers trembled with excitement as she stared down at the wolf. Then he lifted his head she noticed the deep-chocolate eyes.

Her breath caught. Could it be Clint?

She scooted to the very edge of the bench.

The wolf crawled forward a few more inches.

She tried to remember everything she had read about shifters. If she talked to him, would he understand her? Yes! She remembered reading that shifters kept their intelligence. She'd test that theory.

"You are so pretty. Can you come closer? I won't hurt you, I promise."

The wolf moved forward and she gasped in surprise. Did he understand her?

"Do you...?" She stumbled over her words. How could she ask?

The wolf cocked his head to one side and the movement surprised a laugh out of her. She had no doubt he knew what she was saying. She waved her hand, asking the animal to come closer. Finally he was on his stomach right in front of her. She bent and with a shaky hand petted his back.

The hair—or was it fur?—was super soft, much like dogs' fur, and she buried her hand deeper, rubbing harder. The wolf made a sound, something between a moan and growl, but it didn't scare her.

Very carefully, she slid off the bench and down next to him. He remained low and let her guide him to his side.

It was awesome having the wolf laid out like a pet while she ran her fingers over the muscles and toned flank.

"I never would have believed I would be petting a wolf like this," she said.

The animal lifted his head and looked back at her.

"But you're not just an animal, are you?" she questioned.

The wolf shook his head.

"Clint?"

The wolf actually nodded.

She laughed. "Wow!" she said in awe. "This is so cool."

They sat there for a long time, the wolf on his side and her next to him, rubbing his fur up and down. Wow, who needed massages and spas when there was an option to sit out back and pet a wild animal?

Sara couldn't forget, though, that this was also Clint. The man that she was interested in knowing a whole lot better. And he had to have some feelings for her to have come visit in his shifter form. This wasn't the first time, either. She'd seen his silhouette before from her kitchen window. Before, by the time she made it out back, he was gone.

Something had changed, though.

Clint was allowing her to see him. Actually, he was actually giving her a rare gift.

The night got cooler and she shivered. She was disappointed when he rolled back to his feet and stood. He nudged her shoulder with his head.

"I know—I should go in, but this was so cool." She stood and stretched. "Thank you for sharing this with me."

The wolf ran his head under her hand and she patted him.

"I hope to see you for coffee tomorrow?" she told him. She hoped this appearance didn't mean Clint was leaving. Maybe this was his way of saying goodbye or something.

She wanted him now more than ever. And him sharing this secret side had to mean he wanted the same, right? Sara gave him one last stroke before walking inside. At the door, she paused with her hand on the knob and looked back. Clint, still in wolf form, remained in the yard. She smiled and went inside. She locked the door behind her and only then did the wolf turn and trot out of view.

Sara, floating from the wonderful experience, turned off the lights and made her way to bed. She had a feeling that she would be dreaming of Clint again that night.

The house seemed bigger than usual. Sara loved her home, but it was empty most of the time.

Maybe she should get a dog? Did wolves and dogs get along? With Clint in her life, and damn it, he would be, she had to take that into consideration.

She undressed, then slipped beneath the covers, thinking about what an amazing night it'd been. With a smile, she sighed and closed her eyes.

* * * *

Clint stood in front of the coffee shop with Kurt and braced himself to see Sara again. He hadn't planned on letting her see him in his shifter form the night before. He had only been checking on her, making sure no one else was around and watching.

But when he'd caught a glimpse of her standing at the kitchen sink, he hadn't been able to make himself leave. So, he had crouched down as she'd made her way to the door. In his shifted form, he'd been able to see clearly and watch. When she'd started outside, he had frozen, wanting so much to be close to her.

He'd known he was taking a chance. She was human and didn't understand the world he lived in. Clint didn't want to put her in danger, but she'd called out to him. Never before meeting Sara had he felt the intense attraction that swept over him every time he was close to her. He wanted the woman, though he knew it wasn't safe.

Clint opened the door to the coffee shop and stepped inside with Kurt on his heels. The first thing he noticed was the two men from yesterday. They didn't glance in his direction, but they were most certainly aware of him and Kurt. He then noticed that two other tables held patrons who were dressed like the first two men. All the patrons watched him and Kurt openly.

There were no other customers in the place.

Clint looked over to the counter. Sara stood behind the bar talking with her employee, and when she caught sight of him, something like relief spread over her features.

Damn, she was beautiful. Her faded jeans looked soft and comfortable while stretching across her perfect ass.

The short-sleeve shirt she wore under her apron lifted, exposing a small flash of skin, as she nodded and waved over at them.

"Good morning, gentlemen," she greeted.

It was the most formal welcome he had ever received. He frowned and made his way over. Fuck, her hand was shaking, too.

"What can I get for you this morning?" she asked as he stepped up to the counter.

He wanted to reach for her. To reassure her that he would get to the bottom of whatever was going on. He would protect her. Sara was not going to suffer because some assholes had come to her town to talk to the Council.

"Large house blend, please," he murmured, trying to catch her eye.

"Right away," she told him and motioned to her assistant. She placed a napkin on the counter in front of him and turned to Kurt. "For you?"

"The same, please," Kurt responded, glancing between her and Clint, obviously picking up on how strange Sara was acting.

He hadn't said anything to Kurt about his visit to Sara the night before, but if she was wigged out about it, maybe he would need to. He shifted his body and let his gaze wander around the room. The patrons of the coffee shop might be sitting at tables, drinking coffee, but their attention was on the two shifters.

He spun back to the counter and glanced down. The napkin that Sara had placed in front of him had writing on it. Discreetly, he read her note.

They have been here all morning. Every time a customer comes in, they question them about the shifters in the area. It made everyone uncomfortable so they left. Be careful.

Clint slid the note to Kurt and glanced at Sara as she brought the two coffees over. She finally met his eye and he winked. She gave him a small smile in return. Yeah, that was what he wanted to see. Sara wasn't feeling weird about their previous encounter. She was pissed about the men in the shop. He would definitely get rid of them for her.

Kurt balled up the napkin and shoved it into his pocket before pulling out some bills to pay for the coffees. "Thank you," he said to Sara.

She nodded and backed away. The way she blocked her barista spoke volumes to him. Even worried about what was going to happen, she was putting herself in front of someone else.

Clint and Kurt picked up their coffee cups and faced the room.

"So, how was your hunt last night?" Kurt asked loud enough for everyone in the room to hear.

Oh, he was going to love fucking with these guys. Clint shrugged. "Disappointing. There doesn't seem to be much...prey around here."

Kurt shook his head. "That's sad. Maybe that'll change soon."

There was no truth to their threat. They didn't hunt humans, but they had been called evil, so he could see where Kurt was going with this.

Clint eyed the six men in the shop. "I can think of one or...six ideas for that." He gave each man the biggest predatory smile he could.

Several of them paled.

Kurt snorted. "Not much of a challenge."

Clint elbowed his friend and he couldn't help but grin. He was waiting for one of the men to pee himself. "Oh, I don't know about that. We could give them a head start. Drop them off in the middle of the woods and let them think they have a chance at escaping. Maybe we could have our own edition of the *Hunger Games*."

Kurt waved at the two men they'd encountered the day before. "They don't look to be in great shape."

The men huffed and, as their faces reddened, the man farthest from him and Kurt stood. "That is enough!" he snapped.

Clint blinked innocently at the man. "Enough? I have even started yet."

The angry man straightened his tie. "My name is Perry Costa and I work for Reverend Carter. I believe you received my card yesterday and were told of my desire to meet with the shifters of the area, especially the Alpha."

Reverend Dan Carter. The pathetic prick who'd been responsible for the previous attack of his last mission. Clint had been wanting to get his hands on Carter for a long time. He tilted his head. "Perry? Really? I didn't know anyone was actually named Perry. Your parents didn't like you much, did they?"

Clint heard a small giggle from behind him and remembered Sara was still close by. He needed to get the strangers out of there. If any violence broke out, she'd be in danger. And Clint was feeling pretty damn violent.

"Are all of you so…so immature?" Perry questioned, stepping closer.

Kurt snorted. Clint rolled his shoulders, stretching to his full height, causing the man to hesitate. "Guess you just got lucky," Clint replied.

Frowning, Perry narrowed his eyes. "Did you even pass my message along?"

"We did," Kurt replied. "Sorry, no one here is interested in anything you or Carter has to say. Although, I hear the authorities in Riverwood are interested in speaking with him. We'd volunteer to deliver him ourselves, in fact."

Clint grinned at Kurt's reminder that the last time this group had gone after shifters, it had not turned out well for them.

"I would strongly suggest that you let me speak with the person in charge. It has been brought to my attention that you…you people are holding two men against their will," Perry stated. "As a matter of fact, I believe the two of you are the ones who kidnapped the men to bring them here."

"*Kidnapped?*" Clint sputtered. "You're accusing us of kidnapping? That's rich, coming from you. What about the shifter those men we supposedly kidnapped had tied to a chair?"

Kurt gripped his shoulder. Clint hadn't even realized he'd taken a step forward. How dare the man accuse them of kidnapping when it was that group that had kidnapped a friend of theirs from the side of the road and held him against his will?

The only reason Todd hadn't been injured was that another shifter, Mike Jackson, had witnessed it. Clint had been with the shifters when they had rescued Todd. Todd hadn't been injured, thank goodness, and the humans had been arrested. Clint and Kurt had brought the two shifters to the Council to answer for their part in the kidnapping of another of their kind.

Now, at least he knew why the strangers were so interested in him.

"I would hate to have to contact the authorities about this. I believe this is a matter best discussed in private. You have my number. I urge you to let whoever is in charge know I won't be going anywhere. I will speak to them one way or another."

"That sounds suspiciously like a threat," Clint commented with a raised eyebrow. "And please, please, contact the authorities. Or we could do it for you." Inside, he was fuming, but he would not let the man in front of him know that.

"If you truly believed we kidnapped anyone, you would have already called the cops," Kurt added, putting his cup down. "And threatening a Pack of shifters? That's not the smartest move to make."

"You have no idea who you are dealing with," Perry responded. "I hope you will take my warning seriously. Although I don't mind staying in town — great coffee, by the way — I would hate to have these nice people's lives interrupted by this mess."

Clint bit back a growl at the mention of the coffee and the town folk. That was a direct challenge to him. No matter how careful he was from this point forward, Sara was now on their radar. His wolf wanted to tear these men limb from limb.

He needed to think back and retrace his steps. It wouldn't be easy for anyone to spy or follow him. He was a trained shifter. There had to be more to this than Perry and Carter wanting to meet with an Alpha. What was Carter up to this time? He hated not knowing.

Perry rotated on his heel and made his way to the door. The other men followed quickly behind him. Once they were out of the door, Kurt walked over to the window and watched them. Clint turned to Sara.

"You okay?" he asked.

She scooted closer. He smelled the strong coffee scent that seemed to be always with her, and wanted to lean over and sniff her neck. He resisted, barely.

"Yes." She nodded. "It was so weird. They came in right after I opened. Every time another customer came in, they would start asking all these questions, like if they'd seen any shifters and if they knew who was in charge. No one told them anything so those men... They kept getting more aggressive."

Clint laid his hand on the counter and was thrilled when she placed hers in his hold. "It'll be okay. We're already working on it."

"I knew they were waiting on you and I didn't know if I should warn you or not. I didn't like them being in here. They gave me the creeps."

Clint rubbed his thumb over her wrist. "You did great. They're not good people. Have you read about what happened in Riverwood?"

She frowned. "Fires? I think I saw a news report on it a week or so ago."

"Yeah, Carter was trying to bring down one of the oldest Packs. We were sent there to make sure that didn't happen," Clint explained.

"So, he followed you here?"

It was a smart question. "Not sure. It doesn't matter, though. We'll protect this town. It's what we do."

Sara nodded. "I know you'll try, but if these guys are as crazy as they seem... But I also don't want my town burned down."

Clint understood. "I won't let that happen. Where would I get my coffee?"

"Yeah." She laughed. "You remember that."

"Right now they're angling for a meeting. I don't know why. The authorities are searching for Carter, so it's not smart to approach us like this."

"Unless all they actually want is their guys back," she said.

Clint agreed — that was what he was thinking. Even though Carter was against all shifters, he'd used his stepson, a wolf shifter, in his plot against Riverwood. Clint didn't think the shifters who'd failed Carter would live long out of the compound. "We can handle this."

She narrowed her eyes. "You can?"

"Yes." He grinned. "I'm good at my job."

Sara leaned against the counter. "I don't know what that job is, remember."

"Yes." Clint pressed himself against the counter as well. "We should remedy that once this is over."

"That sounds like a great idea," she said. "You know where to find me."

Kurt coughed to get his attention. "We should get back and give an update."

Clint hated to leave Sara, but Kurt was right.

"I'll be back to check on things," he told Sara.

"Promise?" She lifted a brow and smiled.

"Yes." He turned, then strolled out, following Kurt. The street was clear of the men who had been inside the shop.

"Where'd they go?" Kurt questioned.

Clint leaned against the brick wall and just breathed. He used his senses to search the area around him. He could pick up the sound and scent of the residents close by. But there were more. "Two men in an alley a block away. They were at the table next to Perry."

"Okay, anyone else?" Kurt asked.

He tried, but it was much harder to hunt in the middle of a busy street than the woods. Clint shook his head. "I don't know."

"We'll be careful, then. They have to know where the compound is, so as long as we get back there without being attacked, we can let the Council decide how to handle this."

"You got it. And if they do attack?" Clint asked.

"We do what we were trained for," Kurt answered.

Clint had been following under Kurt's command for so long that he didn't question his orders. He trusted his best friend to make the decisions that would keep the two of them alive.

"Let's go let the Council know what's happening," Kurt said.

"You drive," Clint said. "I'll keep an eye out."

* * * *

Stepping inside the compound, Clint heard laughter and glanced at Kurt. Very rarely did anyone come to visit. Plus most of the Council Alphas were so busy they didn't sit around laughing. Kurt grinned and waved him farther into the house.

They walked down the halls and entered the great room, where two Council Alphas sat with three other men.

Kurt whooped and hugged one of the men when he stood. There was a lot of back slapping before Kurt threw his arm around Clint's shoulder and pulled him over.

"Clint, these are some of the most badass Alphas I've ever met," Kurt informed him. "Gage Wolf from West Texas, Austin Winters from Colorado and this guy…" Kurt laughed. "This is Tony. You've probably seen his pretty mug all over the television."

Clint did recognize Tony. He also knew about the two other men. They were highly respected Alphas in the shifter world.

He'd always wanted to meet Tony, too. Tony was the wolf shifter who had become the face of the shifter world. There had been five men total who had stood in place of the all shifters species in front of the public. Those five men had drawn the attention during the announcement of the shifters' existence to keep everyone else safe. All were different species, and Tony had represented the wolves.

Tony had been the perfect choice. He was intelligent, well-spoken and a little bit crafty. His father was also one of the most powerful Alphas in the States and his brother, Cain, was a well-known and highly respected enforcer. Tony had been instrumental in bringing the other shifter species together. The success of the shifters going public was a result of his hard work.

Clint offered his hand to Tony. "Very pleased to meet you," he said.

"Same here. I have heard wonderful things about you and what you've done keeping the Packs safe. We appreciate it."

Clint turned to the two Alphas and shook hands, looking down in respect.

Gage Wolf was an Alpha who all shifters knew about. Talk was, he was already being groomed to join the Alpha Council as soon as he felt his Pack had a good replacement Alpha.

He was also mated to a non-shifter—a woman who had the wolf inside her but could not change forms. Before Gage had mated Marisa, there had not been a lot known about non-shifters. In fact, many, like Marisa herself, had been shunned and kicked out of Packs—some even killed.

Marisa had started an online support group for non-shifters after meeting with a teenage girl from another Pack who was having difficulty dealing with the problems that came from not being able to shift.

The Council had encouraged the Packs to embrace the non-shifters, and Gage had opened his Pack to accept any non-shifter who was not comfortable in their own Pack.

Clint hadn't met a non-shifter himself, but believed in what Gage and Marisa had accomplished.

Gage shook his hand then patted his back. "I met your father several years ago. You take after him."

Clint met the man's gaze and saw the approval. He nodded. "Thank you."

His dad had been an enforcer for the Council for many years before retiring. Clint was very proud of his old man and hoped to follow in his footsteps.

The other Alpha, Austin Winters, was an Alpha of a Pack in Colorado that had decided not to go public. Many of his members had not felt safe with their secret being revealed and Austin had taken that into consideration for his Pack.

He'd also opened up his family and accepted shifters from territories that were going public. Clint had heard he'd gotten almost a dozen new members in only a couple of months.

Austin might not have led one of the Packs that was out in the open, but he remained very supportive of the others who had revealed themselves.

Clint's wolf side wasn't comfortable in the room with such dominant men. The animal side of him wanted to bare his fangs and show his power. It was a good thing Clint could control the wolf, though. For once, he wanted to spend time in the Alphas' company.

"Let's sit and talk about what's going on," Council Alpha Babcock requested.

The men all took their seats before Kurt spoke. "Yes, we have more to add."

While Kurt told them about the morning at the coffee shop, Gage pulled out several manila folders and passed them around.

Clint opened the file to the first page, which was a colorful brochure for *The Church for Humanity* led by Reverend Dan Carter.

"You're kidding," Kurt said, looking disgusted by the name.

Tony frowned. "Sadly, no. Since the mess down in Riverwood, Dan Carter and his followers have been busy. They have opened three chapters of the Church already, inviting humans to band together to oppose the rights given to the shifters. They're even trying to get a law passed, banning any shifter from holding a public office, including any position in law enforcement."

Clint sucked in a breath. He knew several shifters in law enforcement.

"He also wants them banned from joining the military," Gage added.

Clint shook his head. Not only had he been in the army, he had just met another group of shifters who had formed one of the most elite units in the military. That unit had been made up of several different species and had shown how the shifter communities could work side by side with one another.

"They're hitting a lot of resistance. Not only has the government already thought about all of this, some of the officials in charge are shifters themselves," Alpha Conrad said.

"So why are they here?" Clint asked.

"I think they're trying to cover their asses. Dan Carter got ahead of himself and messed up in Riverwood. He has two witnesses who know he's directly involved in kidnapping and arson," Alpha Babcock answered.

"So he wants them back," Kurt stated. "And even though they aren't talking, he doesn't know that."

"Yes, and Carter hasn't been seen. There have been a few sightings but nothing confirmed. He's lying low, but I don't expect him to stay that way," Gage informed them.

"That's not all we have to worry about, though." Austin spoke up. "I had one of my men join the Church. He's been working undercover for a couple of weeks now. While most of the preaching is about protecting their families and children, Colt's told me that's just the public view. He got in with some of the younger crowd and, while the attacks against Riverwood were considered a failure, Dan Carter rewarded the members involved. Promoted them through the program and paid them richly."

"So, it's not over?" Kurt questioned.

Gage sighed. "No, and it's going to get worse before it gets better. Dan Carter is organized and has enough followers that he could cause us a lot of problems."

"Colt and his new friends have been offered a reward if they can capture a shifter," Austin told them. "We've been able to warn the shifters in the area, but that might not be enough. The Church members are getting bolder, traveling farther in their search for a shifter. We can warn the shifters around the areas where the Church is, but if they branch out? We're still a step behind."

"We are trying to get some shifters inside all the Church's chapters, but that takes time and we have to be careful. Dan Carter is also paranoid and checking out all the new members," Alpha Babcock supplied.

"Who's this Perry Costa?" Clint asked.

Gage flipped through his file. "He's Carter's number-one guy. He does the dirty work. If he's here, then they're planning something. Something big. I don't know why he reached out to you but we can't give them whatever he wants."

"Damn," Kurt muttered and Clint had to agree.

"I'll find out where they are staying in town. We'll get a couple of men to follow them, see if we can figure out what their next move will be," Alpha Conrad said. "What they're really doing here. They won't get our prisoners, that's for sure."

"Kurt, I would like you and Clint to talk to the sheriff. He knows what and who we are. Let him know there might be some activity in town. He knows who to trust," Alpha Babcock ordered.

They both nodded.

"We'll take this to the rest of the Council and see what else they think we should do. Gage, Tony and Austin will be staying here while we sort this out," Alpha Babcock said as he stood. "I would like the two of you to take point in town. Let the residents see you, know we're watching out for them. If you need help, give me a call and I can get some of the guards to go down."

After being dismissed, Clint rose and nodded to each man. He was glad he'd been assigned to town. He would be able to keep an eye out for Sara.

Kurt was on his heels as Clint stepped into the hallway. "We'll head to the sheriff's office, then I say we check on your girl again. Maybe have her lie low for a while."

"I don't know if she'll do that," Clint said. The more he learned about Sara, the more he liked her. She wasn't going to let a bunch of bigots run her away from her shop.

"Convince her," Kurt said. "I don't want this turning out like Riverwood."

"It won't," Clint promised. "This town is too good. I like it here."

Kurt clapped him on the back. "I know you do. Me, too."

Chapter Three

Sara juggled the pastry box and cup holder as she pushed open the door to the sheriff's office. She was greeted with a loud holler and the box and carrier taken from her hands.

"Food!" Deputy Gibson cried.

A few years younger than her, Bobby Gibson was the newest member of the sheriff's department. He'd grown up in town and had gone to the university to get his degree before heading back home to the job that Sheriff Webb had for him. Sara had always enjoyed Bobby's excited and friendly personality. Bobby started toward the break table, popping open one of the boxes.

"Oh, man! Muffins!"

She laughed and her dad came out of his office, looking good in his sheriff's uniform, grinning from ear to ear.

"Hey, baby." He hugged her.

"Dad." She laughed. "Do you not feed him?"

Bobby was stuffing his face, waving over the other two deputies who couldn't move because they were laughing so hard.

Her dad shook his head. "I had to call Bobby in early and he didn't get breakfast. Or lunch. He's been moaning over the last two hours that he was wasting away. I was about to send him to the diner."

"Why did you have to call him in?"

It wasn't like they had many crimes in the small town. Every now and then, there might be a small conflict between neighbors or something like that, but since there were always two deputies on duty, they never called for backup.

Her dad patted her back. "Nothing for you to worry about."

Sara tilted her head and scowled at her father. "I brought your favorite, a cappuccino with two raw sugars." She waved to the carrier. "I can smell the espresso from here. It'd be a shame if I took it back."

Her dad sighed and gave in. Just like she knew he would. He might be the big bad sheriff, but she had him wrapped around her finger, had since she was five.

"There are a lot of strangers in town. I wanted to be able to keep an eye out on what was going on," he explained.

She nodded.

"You don't seem surprised," he stated, placing his hands on his hips, giving her the same scowl.

Sara was well-aware they shared that look. She explained what had taken place at the coffee shop earlier and watched his expression grow darker. Of course, she left out a few key things. He didn't need to know about Clint's visits or her feelings for him.

He was muttering under his breath when she finished. "You need to be careful. I got a call from the shifters and they're coming down to speak with me, so until we know for sure what's going on, you need to be on-guard," he told her.

"I will," she promised. "That's why I stopped by. I wanted to tell you about this morning." Sara wasn't stupid. Word would get around eventually and her father would not be happy. Since losing her mom, Sara's dad was very overprotective.

He smiled. "That's my girl." He headed over and stole a muffin from Bobby and picked up the cup of coffee with his name on it.

Sara had learned long ago that being the daughter of the town sheriff came with certain responsibilities. Others looked at her to follow the rules and her dad always worried about his job affecting her. She'd never had any issues.

"So, you want to tell me about this new man who's been coming into your shop?" he asked as he returned to her side.

Well, damn, there really were no secrets in a small community.

"I don't—" she hedged.

"Sara Marie," he warned.

She blew her bangs out of her face. "There may be someone who has caught my attention," she revealed.

"A shifter?" He didn't seem angry or disapproving.

She nodded. "One of the new ones."

He pressed his lips together, then shrugged. "Okay, but that's even more of a reason for you to be careful. With the trouble, you may become a target."

"I guess it's a good thing you've been preparing me for my entire life," she told him.

"You have to remember that I knew about all this. Of course, I made certain you could defend yourself and this town," he said. "Especially if this shifter becomes important to you."

"He already is," she admitted.

"I'll want to meet him. Give him the old 'what are your intentions' talk."

Sara relaxed. Her dad was her everything, her biggest supporter, and she didn't know what she would do if he didn't approve of her getting involved with Clint. Because, after the night before, there was no doubt that she was already involved. She wanted to know him better. To learn all his secrets. It wasn't only the attraction, although that was scorching hot. She just found herself comfortable with him.

The front door opened and she glanced over. She had to blink to make sure her eyes were not playing tricks on her. But, no, Clint walked in with Kurt close behind. As soon as Clint saw her, he smiled brightly before he checked around, then settled his gaze back on her, showing worry.

She glanced over at her dad and saw him watching her and Clint. Well if he hadn't known who the mystery man was before, he certainly did now, if the smirk he wore was any sign. He was going to enjoy this. Even when she'd been in school he'd made certain all the boys knew who her daddy was. No one ever stepped out of line with her. They'd been too afraid of the sheriff.

Kurt reached them first. "Sheriff Webb," Kurt greeted and offered his hand. "I'm Kurt Moore. I'd called you earlier."

Clint looked surprised as he glanced at her over Kurt's shoulder.

Kurt's grin told Sara he'd known Clint had not been aware the sheriff was her father.

"Good to meet you, Kurt," her dad replied. "You must be Clint. I've heard a lot about you."

Clint nodded and they shook hands, too. Clint peered over at her and she understood her father was no doubt making sure Clint's handshake was firm. It would be funny, if she didn't know Clint could probably crush her father's hand if he wanted to. Rumor was that one of the perks of being a shifter was their added strength.

"I was hoping you'd have a few minutes for us," Kurt said to her father.

Her dad looked over at her. "I'll see you later in the week for dinner?"

Every week, she had dinner with him. If he was on call, they met at the diner, and if he was off, he always cooked for her, preferring to grill whenever he had the chance. Even in the winter.

"Yes, Dad," she said and rose to her tiptoes to kiss his cheek.

She passed by Clint and paused.

"You doing okay?" he asked.

She nodded. "Yes, just dropped by to bring some coffee and food to my dad and the deputies. I usually do a couple times a week."

"So nothing else happened?" he questioned.

"No, after you left, it was quiet. A few locals, the book club and the teenagers after school. Normal."

"Good."

"Clint!" Kurt called. "I'm going to go talk to the sheriff. Why don't you keep an eye out for any guests?"

"Yeah, okay," Clint agreed and motioned to the door. "Walk you out?"

Sara was aware that they were being watched as they exited the sheriff's office. Once outside, Clint took a deep breath but stayed close by her side. It looked as though he was trying to sense something. She watched him openly since he had his eyes closed.

"I had no idea your dad was the sheriff," he confessed, still not looking at her.

Sara stiffened. "Is that a problem?" She'd had men not want to date her in the past because her father was sheriff. Yes, he might be a little overprotective, but he was a great guy.

"No," Clint told her before leaning into her. He blinked, appearing to be okay with their surroundings.

She had to tilt her head back to look him in the eye, but his height and strength were a turn-on.

"It eases my mind a little, though. I've been worried that you'll get caught in the middle of what's going on because of me. But I feel better knowing the sheriff's department will watch out for you, too."

"Hmm," she murmured. "And what is exactly going on?" Sara knew that the mission of the humans in town was to keep the shifters' secrets. The shifters in return protected the humans.

Clint's gazed moved over her shoulder. "We're being followed. It's not safe to discuss it here."

She nodded. "Okay."

"Maybe I can stop by later to see you and we could talk about it then?" he asked.

Sara fought not to grin. "I was kinda hoping I would have a visitor later, but he's pure white and on all fours," she teased.

Clint chuckled. "Oh, yeah? I'd like to see that."

"Maybe you will," she replied and stepped back. She needed to leave before she grabbed Clint and gave anyone watching a show. He was acting more respective to her so that was something to look forward to.

Clint stuffed his hands into the pockets of his jeans and rocked back on his heels. "Okay then. I'll be seeing you."

"Yeah." Sara turned and knew that Clint continued to watch her as she made her way to her car. She resisted the urge to look over her shoulder at him. She would see him later and maybe get a taste of what she'd been dying to sample.

On her drive to her house, Sara couldn't help but keep glancing in her rearview mirror. Damn, the men in her life were making her paranoid. There was no other car on the road behind her.

She wasn't far from the compound where the shifters lived.

Only the forest separated the two properties. It made Clint's visits in his wolf form possible, but she needed to think about other people coming through. Her block didn't have a lot of houses. The land the houses sat on was too big. Her closest neighbor was a ten-minute walk.

Usually, she enjoyed the solitude. Sara hadn't noticed any strangers hanging around up there. She'd have to keep a better eye out, though.

She pulled up in front of her house and let out a long breath of relief.

What had she expected? To be attacked in the middle of the road? No, Sara was letting what happened in the shop bother her.

"I'm being ridiculous," she muttered. Sara turned off the ignition before pushing open her door. She'd take a nice, long, hot shower, then make something to eat.

* * * *

There was no sign of Perry Costa or any of his men as Clint and Kurt made the rounds about town. They went into the hardware store, post office, grocery store and finally were sitting at a booth in the back of the diner.

Kurt had filled him in on his conversation with the sheriff earlier, so he knew all the deputies were keeping an eye out for strangers, too. The presence of the deputies might have contributed to the disappearance of their stalkers.

"The sheriff found out they're staying at the hotel, left about noon but didn't check out. They'll be back," Kurt told him.

The waitress came up to the booth with a smile. "You boys know what you want?"

"Coffee and the special, please," Clint requested.

"Same," Kurt added.

She nodded and, snapping her gum, headed back toward the counter. "Coming up."

Clint and Kurt shared a grin. The waitress was older and she wasn't afraid of them. They had become regulars since they'd arrived in town. The easy acceptance they'd received from the people was one of the reasons Clint was so determined to protect everyone.

The waitress stopped back by with piping cups of coffee and set them on the table. Kurt picked his up, thanked her and took a drink.

"Not as good as your girl's shop, but at least it's warm," he noted.

Clint rolled his eyes at Kurt's obvious mention of Sara and the topic he wanted to talk about.

"So..." Kurt pressed when Clint didn't say anything.

Clint leaned forward, bracing his arms on the table. "So?"

Kurt groaned. "Come on, man! What's going on between you and Sara?"

Clint knew Kurt was trying to push him. It was Kurt's way of showing he supported Clint's interest in Sara. But since Clint hadn't decided what to do, he didn't know what to say.

A quick glance at Kurt's face and he knew his friend wasn't going to let him out of talking this time. He took a drink out of his mug, buying himself some time.

He met Kurt's gaze and confessed his deepest concern. "She's human."

Kurt nodded, paused, then narrowed his eyes. "I never thought you'd be the type to ignore an attraction because the other person was human." He rubbed his hands over his face. "That's not right, man!"

Clint stared at his friend in shock, surprised at the outrage. Then it hit him and he started to laugh.

Kurt frowned at him.

The waitress came over and placed two plates of meatloaf, mashed potatoes, green beans and rolls in front of them. Both men thanked her with enthusiasm as the great-looking food made their mouths water. Clint waited until she'd left again before clearing his throat.

"Jeez, Kurt." He shook his head. "I didn't mean it like that."

Sure, there were some shifters who refused to get involved with humans or other shifter species. Clint didn't agree with that way of thinking. He knew Kurt didn't, either.

"What *do* you mean, then?" Kurt questioned.

"I meant that she's human. She barely found out that shifters exist and now all of a sudden she could be in danger because of me. It would only take one person catching on that I have feelings for her and she'll be at risk. They might have already. What if she gets hurt?"

Kurt picked up his fork and pulled his plate closer. "What if she is targeted because her dad is the sheriff? What if you leave tomorrow and they go after her to draw you back? Maybe they'll think she's good-looking and decide they want her to join their fucked-up group."

Clint growled. "You're not helping."

Kurt took a bite before pointing his fork at Clint. "But that's my point. You don't know what is going to happen. You can't guess what will happen in the future. If you want her, you need to make a move before it's too late."

The statement was made by a man who had learned the hard way that sometimes it *was* too late. Kurt had once come close to mating. He'd also just watched his first love meet and commit with another man. Kurt wouldn't appreciate his sympathy, so Clint nodded.

"It's easier said than done," he bitched.

Kurt chuckled. "Oh, I know, man. But I've seen the way you look at her."

"And how is that?" Clint pressed.

"The same way she looks back at you."

Clint sighed. "I know." He'd picked up Sara's strong emotions every time. At least that was helpful.

They went silent as they enjoyed the pleasant meal, both lost in their own thoughts.

Clint had already decided that he needed to discuss his situation with Sara. She had a part in what was going on in town. If she wanted to back away, he would have to allow it. He wouldn't like it, but he wanted Sara to know everything before she got involved with him.

If she decided to trust in him, then Clint would make sure she never regretted it.

"I think you'll be pleasantly surprised by her." Kurt broke the silence a little while later.

Clint glanced up at him.

"Her dad speaks highly of her and her ability to take care of herself," Kurt offered. "She's strong. You need someone who can take care of themselves while being there for you."

Clint dropped his fork and pushed his plate away, stuffed. "And when were you going to tell me that her father was the sheriff?"

"Oh, you didn't know that?" Kurt tried to play innocent and failed by grinning.

"I'll get you back," Clint threatened.

He didn't think his friend was too worried since he just winked and laughed.

Clint turned to look out the diner window. It was getting dark. He could feel the chill starting to settle over the town. He had been looking forward to winter for a while now. He remembered the snow-covered mountains in the distance and the way the entire town celebrated the holidays. Sure, he'd miss not being with his parents or brother, but he'd spent many years beside Kurt. And hopefully this year Sara wouldn't mind if he hung around.

* * * *

Sara made a cup of hot chocolate and hummed while sipping the sweet, comforting brew. A cold front had moved in, finally turning the fall weather toward winter. With colder weather settling around her, she was in her element. Business would be good, and she loved the holidays.

Would this be the year that she would have a special someone to share the season with? She sure hoped so. No matter what happened with the shifters and the strangers who had showed in town, she was determined to get to know Clint better.

Thoughts of Clint made her look out into the yard. She hoped he would still be able to stop by. He'd said he wanted to, and she had teased him about his wolf form.

She wanted him to know that she accepted both his human and wolf side. She might have been ignorant about the shifter world before, but she had no doubt that Clint, Kurt and the other shifters in the area were good, decent people. Her father had been helping them for a lot of years. Her dad wouldn't allow her to get involved with anyone he didn't trust.

Movement and a flash of white caught her eye and she smiled behind her mug.

The big white wolf walked into the backyard before pausing and looking toward her through the glass, and her heart soared. She set her cup down on the counter before rushing to unlock the patio door.

She pulled the door open, and, dressed in only jeans and a sweater, felt the chill of the night hit her. She shivered, but the sight of Clint's tender gaze warmed her. His chocolate eyes were the same no matter what form he was in.

She stepped out onto the wood deck as the wolf crept forward. God, he was so magnificent!

Sara knelt right at the edge of the deck where the wood met grass, and waited until the wolf came closer.

Intelligent brown eyes gazed back at her as she held out a hand.

His fur was as soft as before and she wasted no time in burying her hands and rubbing him. He made what sounded like a cross between a whimper and a moan.

It was a sound she wouldn't mind hearing again and again.

Still in wolf form, Clint stood back up onto four paws and nodded toward the house.

"Would you like to take this somewhere cozier?" she asked.

Sara didn't expect to get an answer so she turned to lead the way inside. She felt movement behind her and glanced over her shoulder to see Clint in human form. He had moved so a tall plant half hid his body. Damn, she had missed it.

But holy cow! The sight of him? She could only see from his waist up but *damn*! He was just as muscular as he looked in clothes but so much more. His flat stomach, small waist and flawless tan skin... She about swallowed her tongue.

Clint must have seen something in her face, because he chuckled. "I didn't know how you would feel about wolf hair in your house. I shed a lot."

She laughed until she had to wipe her eyes. Clint grinned back at her.

"Oh, my God! You really are a wolf shifter," she managed once she got control of herself.

He frowned. "I thought you knew that."

"Well, yeah, but..." She shrugged. How could she explain that knowing and seeing were two different things? "I guess I hadn't thought about you..." She waved her hand at him.

Clint took a step back. "Maybe I should leave."

All her amusement died. Oh, no! No, she didn't want that! "I want you to stay," she confessed.

He nodded. "Okay," he said. "Hang on."

She watched his fine, naked ass—jeez, he was naked!—as he jogged back behind her gate. He was only gone a few minutes, but when he came back he was wearing jeans and a sweatshirt. His feet remained bare, though. She did her best to hide her disappointment that he wore clothes.

He smiled as he joined her back on the deck. "I came prepared."

"I see that." She held out her hand and Clint intertwined their fingers and followed her inside. Sara locked the kitchen door behind them and looked up into Clint's eyes. They sparkled back at her. And her excitement rose.

Almost too suddenly, her desire for him hit her hard. She wanted him, especially after seeing him naked, but now her passion almost swamped her. To have him inside her house… She craved his touch. She cleared her throat, trying to get a handle on herself.

They were only a few feet away from one another. She stepped forward. He did the same.

She lifted her hand to put it on his chest.

Clint placed both of his hands on her face and leaned close. "I've wanted to do this since the first day I saw you," he confessed.

She waited breathlessly as he bent his head. The first brush of his lips against hers was soft. She pressed closer, offering more.

Clint accepted her gift. He sealed his mouth more firmly onto hers, and the kiss deepened. He nibbled on her bottom lip until she opened for him. He begun to make love to her mouth. That was the only way to describe kissing Clint. His tongue massaged hers. and his lips moved softly. If this was what was in store for the rest of the night? Oh, God! She might not survive it.

She had to grab hold of Clint's shoulders as he swept her up in passion and need. She was clinging to him when he pulled back.

"Just as good as I had imagined," he told her.

Sara nodded. "Better," she corrected before lifting up and retaking his mouth.

This time she gave as good as she got, wrapped her arms securely around him and moved their bodies closer still.

She swallowed his moan, humming back at him. Perfect. So damn perfect.

And when the kiss ended, they were both panting.

Sara smiled up at him. "That was so worth waiting for."

He laughed and nodded. "Yeah, it was."

"Would you like to sit in the living room?" she asked, hoping to move them to a more comfortable location. She would have been as happy to go straight to the bedroom, but she didn't want to push him. If it had taken him this long to kiss her, she didn't want to assume too much.

"Yes, I'd love to," Clint said.

"Would you like a drink?"

"Water?" he requested.

She picked up her hot chocolate from earlier and a bottle of water from the fridge before leading the way into the cozy living room.

It was one of her favorite areas. The furniture was old but comfortable, consisting of a large tan leather couch and two matching chairs. The fireplace across from the couch wasn't lit at the moment, but she still liked to sit facing it.

They sat close together and Sara placed her mug on the corner of the coffee table before turning her body toward him.

"Can I...?" She paused, not sure if Clint would appreciate her questioning him.

Clint took a long pull of his water before setting it beside Sara's drink. "What?"

"Can I ask some questions about you?" she asked.

Clint seemed to think about it before nodding. "I'll tell you anything that I can."

Sara took a deep breath. *Well, here goes nothing.* "Do you live here now? Or are you just visiting?"

Clint relaxed back against the couch and smiled. "I have been offered a job here. Well, actually both Kurt and I have been. I am seriously thinking of accepting."

Excitement ran down her spine and Sara leaned forward. "Yeah?"

He leaned closer, too. "Yes."

They kissed and Sara was about to move onto his lap when he pulled back.

"My turn," he told her.

Sara nodded. "Okay, shoot."

"Have you lived here your whole life?" he asked.

Sara wasn't surprised by his question. She'd guessed they would start small and get to the bigger questions as they got more comfortable.

"Most of my life, yeah. I did go to business school down south for a few years, but as soon as I could, I came back. I love this place."

"I can tell that. And can't argue."

"This town... I don't know. We've always lived here. Dad, as you know, is the sheriff. I have a cousin who owns the candle shop. My uncle is the mayor. My aunt runs the community center and most of my friends are still here. It's just home. What about you? Where are you from originally?"

"Not far, actually. About three hours north of here. A small town named Gonzales. My dad worked at the compound when I was a kid. So I visited often. It made sense that when my service was over I would come back here," he explained.

"You have been here before?" she questioned. "Maybe we've met."

Clint moved the arm that was draped over the back of the couch to her shoulder and encouraged her closer. Sara leaned into him and ran a finger down his chest.

"Maybe. When we did visit, we always kept away from most of the locals. I remember the park and my mom used to take me to the library. She was friends with the woman who ran it."

Sara smiled. No doubt Clint was talking about her mom.

"Service? Army, right?" she asked next. She slid her hand over his thigh.

He nodded. "Yeah. It's tradition for my family. My father, uncles and both grandfathers all served."

His voice had dropped in tone as she rubbed his leg, and she was pleased at the husky sound.

"So…" She drew the word out. "Want to see the rest of the house?"

He licked his lips. "Are those all your questions?" He seemed surprised.

"Well, I have enough information to know that I want to move onto the next stage. You won't be taking off in the next few days, so…"

Clint laughed.

Sara frowned up at him.

He shook his head. "I expected a lot more questions. I know shifters are new for you. Most people can't wait to ask about my ability to turn into a wolf."

"I reserve the right to ask any questions later, but I know what I need to right now," she assured him.

"So..." He removed his arm from her shoulder and grasped her hand. "The shifter thing? You're okay with that?"

Sara blinked, caught off guard. She hadn't even been concerned about that. "Oh!" she said. "I hadn't thought about... I mean, is there something to stop us...?" She waved a hand between them. "Can you not be with someone who isn't a shifter?" She was confused. What was Clint doing there if he couldn't be with her? She pulled away.

A look of shock passed over his features before he started to shake his head. "No! No, I just didn't know... I mean I've been with humans in the past, but they didn't know what I was. And as taken as you were with my wolf, I didn't even know if you would want...well, me."

"Okay," Sara stated. She could understand where he was coming from. "But in all honesty, I didn't think about your, uh, animal when we were kissing. I mean, don't get me wrong — I am enthralled with your wolf — but as to spending my night with you... It was you, as a man, that is what I want."

The grin that spread across his face was so strikingly handsome it took her breath away. "I can't tell you how relieved I am to hear that!"

Before Sara could even blink, Clint's mouth was on hers and he had buried his hands in her long hair. He moved over her to lay her back on the wide couch and settled against her body.

Sara was swamped with need as their bodies pressed together.

"Oh, God!" she panted when Clint's hands went under her shirt. That...that felt awesome.

Chapter Four

Clint knew he needed to slow down. The couch in Sara's living room was not the place for their first time together. But he was able to hold back his desire after hearing Sara telling him that it was him, as a man, that she was interested in.

He ground against her softer body while plunging his tongue inside her mouth. His wolf side had awakened and wanted to claim her. Sara shuddered under him and arched into his hands. Clint lifted away enough to push her shirt up and she helped him yank it over her head. He cupped her breasts and squeezed. She responded beautifully. Arching her back and moaning for him, Sara was an amazing sight full of want and arousal. He craved to have her come apart in his hands. To sate the hunger in her eyes.

He bent his head and teased her right nipple through the thin silk material that still covered her.

"Please," she whispered. "I've been dreaming about this."

Clint was glad to give her what she needed. He reached around and unclasped her bra, baring her body to him. Clint dipped his head to start to worship her. He slowly ran his tongue over her firm breasts and playing with her nipples.

She panted under his assault and urged him for more.

Very slowly, he slid his hands down her sides and started to pull the soft cotton pants from her hips. She planted her feet on the couch and lifted to assist him in removing the rest of her clothing. He shifted to the side in order to get the pants and her panties off, then threw them over his shoulder. He reached back and yanked his own shirt over his head so when he moved back over her, flesh met flesh.

The only barrier between them was his jeans. He would correct that soon, but first...first he needed another taste of her.

He settled between her legs and kissed her again. He didn't think he would ever get tired of the flavor of her. He licked at the roof of her mouth while running his hands over her, mapping her body, familiarizing himself with every inch of her.

Sara gripped his sides, her nails digging in a little, and bucked up into him. His erection was so hard, straining against his zipper, Clint didn't know how much longer he could hold back. This wasn't how Clint had been picturing their first time together. His usual control was slipping from him.

"Don't be gentle," Sara whispered.

Clint stilled.

"I'm not some delicate flower you have to hold back with."

He peered down at her. Her eyes were full of passion. Clint wasn't sure that she even knew what she was saying though.

"I mean it." Sara reached up to brush his cheek with the back of her hand. "I know what I'm asking. It will take trust on both our sides. Take a chance."

He was too desperate to have Sara to deny either of them. Decision made, he grinned. She smiled back.

Clint brushed his fingers between Sara's folds and, finding her slick and wanting, pressed one digit into her.

"Uh, Clint, please," she begged.

Such a sweet sound.

He plunged his finger in and out, loving the way her hips lifted with him. His cock had been hard all night, but now if he didn't get inside her soon, he would come in his jeans. He didn't want that to happen.

Inside, his wolf half was clawing at him, need and want driving the animal into a frenzy.

"Clint!" she cried.

"Baby," he murmured against her neck as he added a second finger inside her.

"I need you," she told him, pressing up and digging into his back before reaching to his front.

Clint gasped as she cupped his erection through his jeans. Fuck, he almost came right then.

She rubbed him harder, drawing a low long moan from him. She undid the button of his pants and Clint rose onto his knees so he could help Sara get his jeans down. Once his pants were past his hips and to his knees, he kicked enough to get them off.

He urged Sara's legs up toward her chest and lowered his face to tease her sweet pussy. She cried out and clutched his head. The bite of her nails against his scalp spurred him on.

Clint loved the scent and taste of this woman. Sara was also vocal. He liked that in a lover, knowing that he was pleasing his partner. He spent a few minutes satisfying her until she was shaking and almost sobbing. Then he scooted closer and placed himself against her center, his cock positioned and ready to claim her.

"Look at me," he ordered and she raised her gaze to his.

Eyes locked on hers, he slowly entered her.

She was hot. Hot and wet, and as he pushed inside, so damn good and tight.

He pulled out and their moans mixed together.

He thrust back inside and was in heaven. Gently, he started to love her. In and out, hard short strokes, until he couldn't control himself and started to plunge inside.

The slap of skin against skin filled the room as they rocked together. Sara met him stroke for frenzied stroke and scored her nails down his sides. The little bite of pain almost sent him off and he levered up enough to pound into her.

"Yes!" she screamed and her inner muscles clamped down as she climaxed.

"Fuck!" Clint didn't slow down. He rocked himself faster. With the firm grip he had on her thighs, he felt each tremor of her body. Even though he was close, Clint needed to release the animal he'd been holding back.

With a shout, he allowed the wolf to the surface. He didn't transform, merely let his senses flow. With shifter speed, he was able to take Sara to a whole new level.

Clint roared. He came hard. Spots formed in front of his eyes as he emptied into her.

Sara was calling him name in pure ecstasy.

He collapsed on top of her, trying to catch his breath.

"Holy shit!" she said with a laugh.

He roused himself to look at her face. "I didn't hurt you, did I?"

Sara ran her hand over his cheek. "That was the most amazing thing I have ever experienced."

Clint's heart soared. God, he could fall for this woman. He rocked his hips very gently. He was still half-hard buried inside her, asking without words for more.

She raised an eyebrow. "Oh, hell, yeah," she said and reared up before she latched her mouth to his.

Even with the sweat covering both their bodies, Clint didn't care. Her hand slipped off his back to lay flat on the upholstery of the couch.

"I think we can do better than this," he told her. Clint withdrew, chuckling when she whimpered and reached out to him. He caught her hand before pulling her up and over his shoulder.

"What...are you doing?"

"I think we need a shower before we find your bed," he said.

"Okay." She slapped his ass. "Do I have to hang upside down?"

"I like you like this," he commented.

She grumbled something that even his enhanced hearing didn't pick up.

Sara's house was how he'd pictured it. The comfort and warmth surrounding him as he walked down the hall called to the place inside him that craved having a home of his own.

"This door." She waved her hand and Clint turned to the open door. Inside was what appeared to be the master bedroom. Done in warn tans and browns, Sara's room also had a large bed in the middle. He wanted to deposit her on top of the mattress but their shower needed to come first.

"Bathroom straight ahead," she told him.

Clint continued strolling forward. Reaching the entry, he slid her down his body until they were once again pressed up against each other.

Sara threaded her fingers with his and tugged. "Come on."

He entered the small blue-and-white-tiled room and grinned. There was no tub, just a large standing shower that would be big enough for the two of them. Clint sauntered over to turn on the shower while Sara pulled down towels from a cabinet.

"I hope you like it hot," he said.

"With you? It'd better be steaming," she replied.

He grinned. She walked over, then trailed her fingertips over his chest. "Come wash my back."

Clint followed her into the stall. Closing the door behind them, he turned to Sara. She was already under the spray with the water running over her body. If he'd ever seen a more gorgeous sight, Clint couldn't remember.

* * * *

Clint groaned as he came awake. Absolute and undeniable pleasure coursed through him as his raging morning hard-on was taken inside a warm wet mouth.

He lifted his head to peer down at Sara, who took his length into her mouth again.

She gazed back at him, never stopping the amazing blowjob.

He threaded his fingers in her hair, stroking and encouraging her.

Sara sucked hard and that was all it took. Clint gasped, then was coming. She pulled back while finishing him off with her hand. Clint reached for her hand to bring her up as soon as his body stopped responding.

Clint kissed her deep and she responded with enthusiasm. He didn't know how he'd gotten so lucky. If Clint hadn't been sent to Riverwood, then ordered to bring the guilty shifters to the Council, it could have been months or years before he returned and met Sara.

Looking up, she smiled at him.

Clint almost felt guilty at how bad he wanted to wrap himself around Sara and never let her go. The possessiveness was new and a little bothersome.

"Did you sleep okay?" she asked.

He nodded, unsure how to express what he was feeling.

"Me, too," she said. "And waking up with your arms around me was perfect. You were holding me so tight. Like you didn't want me to disappear."

"I'm sorry," he managed. "Did I hurt you?"

She laughed. "Did you not hear me say it was perfect?" she asked. Sara smacked his chest. "Do you need coffee?"

Clint laughed. "First, I need you." He rolled her over and onto her back. Covering her body with his, he began to play.

Sara stretched out, her skin glowering in the morning light, pulling at him. Clint kissed down her neck and his fucking cell phone rang.

"No!" he wailed.

She giggled. "At least we remembered to charge our phones last night."

He sighed. Sara had an extra charger so he'd been able to plug his phone in. Now he regretted it. "That's Kurt's ringtone."

"Answer it," she said. "It's fine."

Clint grunted but reached for his cell. "Hello?" he said, not without frustration. He was horny again and Sara hadn't gotten off yet.

"I need you back at the compound," Kurt said.

"Now?" he said.

"Yes, the Council called a meeting."

Clint looked down at Sara. "Fine."

She nodded back before patting his chest. Clint sat up.

"I wouldn't have called you if I didn't have to," Kurt said. "I'm guessing since you didn't return home last night you're still in bed with..."

Clint growled. "Don't go there."

Kurt laughed. "Just get back. I'll wait at the back door."

"On my way." Clint pressed Disconnect before tossing his phone onto the mattress. "I have to go."

"I figured." Sara had already pulled on a pair of sweatpants and a tank top.

"I'm sorry our morning got interrupted." He grabbed her hand to draw her between his legs.

"I guess you'll have to make it up to me," she teased.

"Oh, I will," he promised. "Tonight?"

"Please."

73

"I'm going to shift and run back. Can I leave my bag and clothes here?" he asked.

"Sure," she said.

Clint rose before taking her hand and leading her toward the back door. He was going to shift in front of her and trust that she could handle it.

He took a deep breath as he reached the back door. This was where thing could go wrong. She enjoyed seeing him as a wolf, but what about the change? Would that freak Sara out?

"Hey." She pulled him to a stop. "I can see you're anxious. I want to watch, but if you'd rather shift in private, I understand."

"I don't mind. Just remember that it's still me."

"Of course, I will," she replied.

Clint gave her one last kiss, making sure it was full of all the feelings he hadn't voiced. When he pulled back, she was gasping for breath. Oh, yeah, he still had it.

He opened the back door and stepped naked out onto Sara's beautiful deck. There was still moisture in the air from the cold front coming in the previous night. He turned and winked before dropping to his knees. It was too chilly to waste time. With Sara standing in the doorway, he called forth his wolf form.

The change rippled over him, and in a few minutes, he was seeing the world differently. He glanced up and saw that Sara had gone to her knees. She was smiling at him.

He shook out his coat before tromping over. Sara didn't hesitate to scratch his ears.

"I'll see you tonight," she said. Then she placed a kiss on the top of his head. "Go."

He nodded, then took off. Her gate was still open so he raced through it into the forest that separated Sara's and the Council's properties.

It didn't take long. Clint had made the trek so many times that the route was familiar. As promised, Kurt stood outside the back entrance with a handful of clothes. Clint ran to him and before Kurt knew what was happening, he barreled into his best friend.

Kurt cursed. "Damn it!" He finally laughed.

Clint lifted his front paws to Kurt's shoulders to lick his face.

"Ugh!" Kurt pushed him down. "Knock it off."

Since there was work to do, Clint didn't annoy his buddy any more. Instead, he settled down to transform back to his human form.

"What's up?" Clint questioned, once he could talk. His voice was still a little rough and he needed to eat, but he was curious as to what had happened.

Kurt waved him to follow and Clint did. They went into the same room they'd been in before and he saw Tony was already inside, pacing.

"Hey, thanks for getting up early," Tony said and shook their hands.

"No problem," Kurt said.

Tony motioned for them to sit. Gage and Austin entered with a tray full of coffee cups.

Coffee was passed around and Clint couldn't help but compare the brew to what Sara had served earlier. It didn't even come close to Sara's. He hid his smile behind his cup.

"Colt called last night," Tony explained. "He and some of his new friends will arrive this morning."

Kurt sat back and raised his eyebrow. "That's quick."

Tony nodded. "They've been told there are two shifters here causing the town problems and they need to be captured. Colt said his man got word from Perry Costa."

"So, Perry is still running the show here? No sign of Dan Carter?" Kurt asked.

"And we're the two shifters they're coming after?" Clint inquired.

"Yeah, no word from Carter, and they were given pictures of the two of you."

"What are the orders?" Clint questioned.

"Capture, alive," Tony told them.

"At least they didn't say to shoot us on sight," Kurt stated.

Clint grinned at his friend. Capture? Oh, that wasn't going to happen. There was a reason that Kurt had headed his own unit in the army and why Clint was one of the top hunters in the world. They worked well as a team.

Gage's chuckle drew Clint's attention.

"From the looks on your faces, I take it you're good with being bait?" the Alpha asked.

Clint and Kurt both nodded. "Of course," Kurt responded easily.

"Crazy-ass bastards," Austin murmured under his breath. Everyone chuckled.

"Colt's going to try to keep us appraised as best he can, but he can't blow his cover. So unless your life is threatened, he won't step in. You'll be on your own," Tony told them.

Tony drew out his phone and clicked a couple of buttons before he handed it over to Kurt. Kurt took a quick look, then passed the phone to Clint. Clint glanced down.

"That's Colt," Tony told them. "So at least you'll know who he is."

The picture was of a young, attractive man sitting at a table with a mug of beer in front of him. The man was smiling into the camera, obviously happy with life. Clint handed the phone back to Tony, who took it and glanced back at the picture. The soft expression on Tony's face drew his attention. Clint recognized the look. He'd seen it plenty of times. Maybe not on his own face but on others.

Tony was in love with Colt.

He wondered if Colt knew or if he felt the same way. Being gay wasn't anything that bothered Clint and he knew Kurt would feel the same. Kurt's brother Kenny was in a relationship with another man and they both respected the hell out of Todd – the shifter who Dan Carter had kidnapped in Riverwood.

"As much as we want to get to Dan Carter, we need to treat Perry Costa as a threat. He's obviously in charge here," Austin added to the conversation. "Colt's never even met Carter. But Carter's son Bruce is coming down with Colt's group, so that is going to put a lot of heavy power in one place. They have to be planning something big."

Silence fell.

"There's more," Alpha Babcock stated as he joined them.

Gage stood and offered his seat to the Council Alpha, but Alpha Babcock waved him back down.

"I'm on my way to a meeting with the other Council members. I wanted to let you know that I just received a call from one of my guards in town. About fifteen minutes ago, the Church members began to show up in town."

"How many members?" Gage asked.

"Around thirty or so," Alpha Babcock answered. "And carrying protest signs."

"They're staging a protest in a town where they don't even live?" Clint inquired.

The Council Alpha nodded. "Yes, and the publicity is a concern. That's why a meeting has been called."

Tony stood. He walked over to the large bay window. "What exactly are they hoping to do?"

No one had an answer for him.

Alpha Babcock cleared his throat. "I'll give you a call later."

Austin stood and went over to Tony. He placed a hand on Tony's shoulder and spoke to the other man quietly. Things were moving fast and no matter what the Carter's orders were, it was Clint's job to ensure that everyone remained safe. The town of Lovington was supposed to be a place where humans could live without any fear. Now, Carter's church was upsetting an agreement that had been working for many years.

"It could be a way for us to give in. Bring in the protesters and cause bad publicity for us until we agree to meet with them," Clint offered. He was never that lucky, though.

"But if they want the two shifters that we brought up here, why would they want the attention? They can't pull anything off if we're being watched. It puts their own mission more in the open," Kurt argued.

"That's what I can't get a handle on. When Perry Costa first appeared, he mentioned the two men we have in custody. But when he sent Colt and the others here, he didn't mention them. Just wanted you and Kurt captured," Gage said with a growl of frustration.

Tony and Austin walked back over and joined them. Tony's expression was calm again. The man who'd fought the hardest to allow the shifters to become public deserved to catch a break. Clint would look out for Colt. Make sure that he returned home to Tony.

"You okay?" Clint asked Tony. He didn't want to pry but hoped Tony knew if he needed anything, Clint would help.

Tony nodded and offered him a small smile. "It's maddening. We worked so hard to make sure when we went public we were treated properly. We have the government behind us. Have friends in high places. Still Dan Carter is getting away with too much."

"Hey, you did awesome bringing us all together," Kurt assured Tony. "I was proud to have the wolves represented by you. We'll take care of this mess and everything will be fine."

"Then we need a plan," Tony stated. "Let's get this over with."

Clint couldn't agree more. He had plan for later that night and he wasn't going to let Dan, Perry or any other bigot stop him from being with Sara again.

"Austin needs to stay out of sight," Gage stated.

Austin snorted in response. "I appreciate you trying to hide my identity, but I'm in this. If I'm needed, I won't hold back."

"You have your Pack to worry about," Tony said.

"And they'll understand. Don't worry about me," Austin countered.

"Fine," Kurt said. "Austin is out unless we need him. Clint and I will see about making more waves. If they want us, then they're going to get us, all of us."

Clint nodded. "I'm up for some fun."

* * * *

Sara couldn't believe what she was seeing. The small, quiet town she called home was overrun with people she had never seen before, holding up signs and chanting. There were protesters in the streets in front of her shop and the other stores on the block.

She glanced over at Cecil as they watched from the front window.

Cecil shook his head. "I can't believe this," he whispered. "Who are all these people?"

Sara wasn't sure why he was whispering, but she nodded. It was an unbelievable sight. "I don't know."

Men, women and children were marching in the street and on the sidewalks, signs against shifters moving up and down, and every time someone walked or drove by, they would call out to try to get them to join in.

The coffee shop was empty. In fact, other than a few cars and some brave souls, the streets were almost deserted of locals. She turned her back to the window and stalked to the counter, her temper rising. She slammed her hand down. This was crazy. Surprised when the front door opened, she whirled around. She had no intention of serving any of the protesters and prepared to turn the person down for service.

"Dad!" She waved him over. "What is all this?"

He shook his head, pulling at the collar of his uniform shirt. "Absolute bullshit. And one of my guys called over the radio and said news vans were headed this way."

"The news?" she gasped. "Damn, those aren't even residents out there!" Anger had her clenching her fists.

"Don't you get involved," her dad ordered, pointing a finger in her direction.

She didn't know what he'd seen on her face, but she couldn't make him any promises. She wished she had Clint's number. That was number one on her list the next time she saw him. Okay, maybe a kiss first, but then right after, she was getting his number. She hated to think that he might believe the residents were actually involved with this circus.

"I've already spoken with Kurt. They know what's going on and want us to do our best to ignore it," he said. "He hopes the residents will stay away from this clusterfuck. I'm going store to store to help make that happen."

This was something not likely to be ignored. But it also wasn't her place to push. "Coffee?" she asked.

He nodded and she began making his grande cappuccino with two raw sugars. Her dad grinned wide when she handed it over.

"I've got to get back out there," he said. "I hope one of them does something illegal so I can arrest them."

With that said, her dad waved and left. Cecil laughed and went to start sweeping up. Sara began cleaning the espresso machine. They'd been right smack in the middle of the morning rush when the protesters had lined up outside. Everyone had stood around in shock and just stared. Sara had walked outside with several of her customers while the first protesters had launched into their chant. What had astonished her most were the young children holding up signs and repeating the words of hate their parents were yelling.

That... It was wrong.

She was scrubbing the stainless steel steaming wand when the door opened again.

Six young men walked in and took a look around. Unease traveled up her spine and she darted a glance over to Cecil. Her employee looked back at her, wide-eyed, and scurried back to stand by her.

Cecil might be young, but he wasn't stupid. He'd had a hard life already and Sara was very protective of him. She shifted forward enough that she would be the focus of the strangers.

One of the guys strolled toward the counter, staring at Cecil.

"Hey, pretty boy," he said. "What're you selling?"

Cecil shook his head and backed up.

"Can I help you?" Sara asked.

The man's gaze went to her. He looked her up and down before he lifted his lip in disgust. "You the shifter slut?"

"Excuse me?"

He laughed, a nasty sound that grated her nerves and fit the horrible man.

"You need to leave," she stated and crossed her arms over her chest.

He snorted. "You gonna make me? Or maybe the pretty boy behind you is?"

Sara was almost shaking, she was so pissed. "Yeah, yeah, I am." She'd started around the counter when another man stepped forward.

"Come on, Rudy," he said. "Let's get out of here. The sheriff might come back."

Rudy, the arrogant prick in front of her, frowned before looking over his shoulder at his friend. "You scared, Colt?"

The other man, Colt, dropped his head and shrugged.

"Pussy," Rudy spat out, then turned back to Sara. "I'm here to give your boyfriend a message."

Sara didn't react. Clint had said he had been followed, so it shouldn't shock her that these men knew about her relationship. But if they thought they could use her to get to Clint, they had another think coming. She wasn't some helpless female who was going to go cry to Clint.

"Tell him that I'm coming for him. Gonna take him down like the animal he is."

Sara glared at his back as the men left her shop. The one named Colt was the last to leave. He turned and winked. Sara sputtered. He lifted his finger to his lips in a *be quiet* gesture. She lifted her eyebrow in response.

Then the door was closed behind him.

"What was that about?" Cecil asked.

"I have no idea," she replied. There had been something in the guy's expression that made her think that Colt wasn't like the men he'd been with.

Chapter Five

Clint searched his phone for the number of the coffee shop just as he and Kurt walked into the alley. They'd left the compound by the hidden exit before making their way to town. It appeared no one had spotted them and, with the protesters drawing attention to themselves in town, Clint and Kurt did their best to remain unseen.

He hit Connect and waited for someone to pick up the phone.

Sara answered with a friendly 'hello' and he felt immediately calmer. He had worried about how she was doing. The perfect morning had been spoiled by the arrival of Dan Carter's people.

"Hey, beautiful," he greeted her.

Kurt smirked beside him, and Clint turned away.

"Clint!" The relief in her tone was evident.

"Come open the back door for us," he requested.

"You're here?" she asked. "Is that safe?"

He chuckled. "Well, it would be better if you would come open the door."

"Oh!"

He shared a look with Kurt as they heard the lock being undone and the door opened. Sara stuck her head out with the phone still held up to her ear.

"Hurry." She motioned them inside.

Once they were through, she slammed the door closed and locked the dead bolt. She threw her arms around his neck. "I was so worried about you! That man! He said he was going to get you and I — "

"Hey! Hey! It's okay." He wrapped his arms around her waist and held her tight. "What man? What are you talking about?"

She shuddered and he pulled away enough to look down at her face. Something had happened and he clenched his jaw in anger.

"These guys came into the shop earlier. They were...horrible — well, one guy, anyway — and he said to give my boyfriend a message," she explained.

Kurt stiffened beside them.

"He said to tell you that he's coming for you. Gonna take you down like the animal you are. Those were his exact words," she finished.

"Hey." He caressed her cheek. "I'm okay." He wasn't surprised that they'd contacted Sara. Without him out in the open, Perry's group didn't have any other avenue. Maybe he could talk Sara into closing the shop for a few days. That'd been Kurt's idea, but Clint doubted she would.

She nodded, then closed her eyes while leaning against him.

"What else did they say?" Kurt asked. "What did they do?"

They were still standing in the dark hall. Sara looked toward to the front.

"I...I don't want to leave Cecil alone. That man, he kept calling Cecil 'pretty boy', and I didn't like the way he was looking at him."

Clint pressed his lips together. The times that Clint had been coming into the shop showed him Cecil was a great kid. It was also obvious how protective Sara was of him. "Let's sit out front and have some coffee and talk," he suggested.

"Out front? Are you sure? What if those men return?" Sara tugged where her hands were wrapped in his shirt.

He kissed her forehead. "Trust me, baby. Come on." He led the way down the hall and when he pushed the swinging door open to enter the front of the shop, Cecil looked up.

"You okay?" he asked.

Cecil bobbed his head up and down.

"Okay, let's get a couple of coffees and sit."

Cecil rushed over to the counter and started lining up cups.

Kurt moved to the closest table to the counter and sat in the chair that faced the front door. Clint sat beside him and angled his chair where he could cover the back. Sara sat next to him and he couldn't help but run his gaze over her.

"Hi," he said.

She smiled. "Hi."

Cecil cleared his throat and set the cups of coffee down. "Here you go."

Clint lifted his cup and took a drink. "Oh, man, I needed a cup of the good stuff."

Kurt grunted in agreement, then turned toward Sara. "Tell us everything."

He listened as Sara told them what had happened from the moment the six men had entered the shop until they'd left.

He picked up on the two names that were provided. Rudy and Colt. Since Colt had already given them the names of the men he was hanging with, it matched everything they knew. So, Colt and his group had arrived in town. She'd also been curious why Colt had been acting different. Clint didn't tell Sara about Colt because they were in public, but he'd make sure to mention it later. She needed to know they had an inside man and that Clint would never let anyone hurt her.

"Kind of stupid to give us a warning," Clint shared with Kurt.

"Yeah," Kurt concurred.

"Stupid! They threatened you!" Sara cried.

"Hey!" Clint grasped her hand and pulled her closer. She slid into his lap. "We know what we're doing," he assured her.

"But—" she started to argue.

"Sara…" He cupped her cheek. He hated to see the worry on her face. "This is what we do. We protect people. If they're after us, then we know everyone else is safe."

She rested her forehead against his. "I don't want anything to happen to you."

"It won't," he promised.

She sighed but nodded. "I trust you."

"You don't seem surprised that these men came looking for you," Cecil accused.

"We're not," Kurt responded. "We'd already heard that there were men headed this way. We've got it handled."

Cecil shook his head. "Hope so, man. That Rudy guy…" Cecil shuddered. "He gave me the creeps."

"Hey, kid," Kurt said. "You be careful. Watch your back and don't go out at night alone. They aren't after you, but don't take any chances. Don't try to engage them for any reason."

Cecil smiled. "I'm no hero. I'm not going to draw attention to myself, trust me."

"Good." Kurt reached for his wallet and pulled out a card. "That's my number. You see anything that makes you uncomfortable, call me or Clint. One of us will be right there."

Cecil looked reassured and slipped the card into his back pocket. "Thanks."

"Same with you." Clint kissed the tip of Sara's nose. "They obviously know about us. I don't want you to take any chances."

She shrugged. "I doubt they'll try anything against the sheriff's daughter."

He grasped her chin and made her meet his gaze. "I mean it, Sara."

"I promise I'll be careful," she offered.

It wasn't the assurance he wanted, but he decided not to push it for now. "Okay."

Kurt stood and motioned Cecil away from the table.

Once they were alone, Clint dipped his head and placed a kiss against her lips. "Last night and this morning?" he started. "Those were some of the best moments I've ever shared with anyone. I want more of them. Which means you need to let me handle this and not get hurt."

"I understand," she replied. "I want more, too."

"I'll let you know what's going on. I'll try to stop by tonight."

"Yeah?" She wiggled on his lap.

His cock hardened. "Oh, yeah," he responded before kissing her deep.

She hummed and opened for him. He ran his hands down her face, around to caress her neck, before he dug his fingers into her shoulders.

She moaned into his mouth.

"Damn, honey," he said when they broke apart. "We'll have to pick this up later."

She looked up at him, her face flushed. "Later."

He stood but couldn't resist one more kiss. "Call if you need anything," he ordered, then squeezed her hand and followed Kurt through the swinging door to the back.

Kurt stayed silent as they made their way back out to the alley. Once out into the bright, cool day, Clint pulled on his sunglasses.

"Ready to hunt?" Kurt inquired.

"Oh, yeah," Clint chuckled. "Let's get this party started."

* * * *

Sara stepped out of the front door of her shop with Cecil and locked up.

The protesters were still out on the street. Several of them were giving interviews to the reporters who stood with cameras and microphones. Those people didn't even live there!

"Look around," she said softly to Cecil. "You see the creeps?"

Cecil was quiet a minute before she heard his breath catch. "Yeah," he murmured. "In front of Walker's Second-Hand Clothing."

Walker's was the clothing store most of the older residents shopped at. It was across the street and two doors down. She put her arm through Cecil's and pulled him with her. They had to dodge through the protesters that were still gathered.

"Don't look at them. Don't respond," she told Cecil as some of the crowd yelled.

They reached the front of her cousin's store and she pushed Cecil toward the door. She glanced over her shoulder and saw that they were being followed.

The men weren't exactly hiding, so she figured they didn't care if they were spotted.

The candle store that her cousin Linda owned was one of Sara's favorite places. She loved the smell, but it was the homey feel that made the store one of the most popular in town.

Not only did Linda sell homemade candles, she also sold local art. The art was a combination of every imaginable way people expressed themselves. Sara had several pieces in her home.

"Hey, cuz. Hey, Cecil," Linda greeted as they stepped inside.

Sara waved and pulled out her cell phone. Cecil headed to the register to start talking to Linda. Sara went to where she had programmed Clint's number into her phone and pressed the Call button.

He picked up on the second ring.

"We're being followed," she told him after he answered.

"I know. I'm watching," he replied.

Of course, he was — she should have figured that. But it did make her feel better that he was there. Even though he was the real target.

"Good job ducking into the store there. Are you safe inside?"

"Yeah, it's my cousin's shop," she explained.

"Okay, good. Kurt and I both have eyes on our visitors. Once you leave there, I want you to head to the sheriff's office. We'll stay right behind you. Don't act like you know anything is going on."

She sighed and rubbed her forehead where she was starting to get a headache. "Okay."

"Kurt's calling your dad," he continued. "We'll have him take you and Cecil home. Once you get there, lock your door and keep your phone close. I'll call up to the compound and make sure one of our guys is watching the house. I don't think they'll follow you home, but we'll be careful."

"All right." She tried to take deep breaths and calm her pounding heart.

"Nothing will happen to you. I promise."

"I'm taking Cecil home with me. He lives in an apartment right off Main Street, but I don't want him alone," she said.

"Good idea," Clint told her. "You two stay together. Go to the sheriff's office and meet your dad. I'll be watching, honey."

"Thanks," she said. "Thanks, Clint."

"No problem. I'll talk to you soon." After he hung up, she felt ten times better. She joined her cousin and Cecil and they talked for a couple of minutes. She bought some candles so it looked like they had entered for a reason before she and Cecil headed toward the door.

She explained to Cecil what the plan was and he grinned.

"You sure my being there won't ruin your" —he cleared his throat—"plans for the night?"

She hip-checked him as they went outside. Cecil's laughter made her feel lighter.

They kept their heads close together and spoke quietly as they made their way to her dad's office.

"God, I wanna look so bad," Cecil confessed.

Sara giggled. "Me, too."

It was hard to resist. She was so damn curious to see if the men were still there, if she could pick Clint out of the crowd. They made it into the sheriff's office and, when she stepped inside, she could see that it was packed. The deputies seemed harassed and had their hands full with several people yelling about their rights. Her dad stepped through the crowd and motioned them forward.

She ducked between people and they rushed into his office.

"Pieces of shit," he muttered, slamming the door closed.

Sara swallowed back her laugh. It took a lot to get her father to go off, but when he did, it was always astounding.

"We've wasted an entire day arresting these idiots for one petty crime or another. Did you know they knocked down old lady Carmen when she tried to chase them off her property with a broom?"

"Damn it," Sara cursed. Anna Carmen was the oldest resident in town at ninety-three years old. She was a spirited woman and Sara loved her. "Is she okay?"

He grinned. "Takes more than that to keep her down. Boy, was she pissed, though."

Sara could only imagine. "I'll call and check on her tonight."

He nodded. "Kurt called and updated me. Do you think you'll be okay at home?"

"Yeah, Clint was going to have someone watching the house."

He looked surprised, then nodded. "He's a good guy. Really good guy," he said.

Sara smiled. "Yeah," she agreed.

"Well…" He cleared his throat. "Let's get you two home, then."

They followed him through the side door out of his office and into his truck. They stayed quiet during the drive. Her dad darted looks to the rearview mirror every few seconds.

He pulled up in front of the house. "Stay in here while I check everything out," he ordered.

"But, Dad…" she argued, but one look and she closed her mouth. She knew that look.

He climbed out of the truck, slammed the door, then walked up the porch to the front door and used the spare key he carried to enter.

He was only gone about five minutes or so, but it seemed much longer. Her hand was on the door handle just in case.

She relaxed when he came back out onto the porch and waved at them.

Both Sara and Cecil climbed out of the truck so they could hurry inside.

"Lock the door," her dad ordered.

"Yes, Dad."

He leaned over and kissed her cheek. "Love you. Keep your phone with you at all times."

"Love you, too," she told him.

Once he had started down the steps, she closed and bolted the door.

She turned around to Cecil, who was standing in the hall. "Movies and popcorn?"

Cecil grinned. "I pick the first one!"

* * * *

The six men split up after Sara had left the sheriff's office with her dad. Clint expected at least one group to follow her, but while he followed three men around town, Kurt called him and informed him that the other group was hanging around the woods by the compound.

Clint's group contained their contact to Colt and two other young men. They walked behind the protesters, hung around the park and basically didn't do a whole hell of a lot. He had called Sara and checked in with her. All was fine there. The Alphas had had no problem sending one of the guards to watch her place, so that made him feel better.

But he was bored.

Not that he was looking forward to any trouble, but he wished they would get on with whatever the plan was. He would much rather spend his time getting to know Sara than stalking a bunch of humans. He was leaning back against one of the alley walls, keeping his eye on the men, when he saw Tony and Austin walking around in the park.

Colt stiffened when he spotted the two men.

Tony and Austin were in jeans and T-shirts, heads down, blending into the crowd. Clint wasn't sure what was going on, but he didn't like it. Tony was one of the most public faces the shifters had. If even one person recognized him, there could be a riot. Clint straightened and moved closer to the edge of the crowd. If there was trouble he wanted to be ready. Austin and Tony had almost reached Colt and the other men. Clint watched Tony meet Colt's gaze. Tony was even so bold to wink.

Colt looked furious.

Austin and Tony passed by without a word to any of the men. Clint shook his head. *Man.* Tony and Austin had balls of steel. He followed their movements until they were back to their SUV and had climbed inside. He wasn't sure what that appearance had been about, but he planned to ask later when they all met up again. He turned his attention back to the three men he was supposed to be watching. They had settled onto a bench in the park. Clint relaxed back against the building.

Clint remained there for another hour before one of the men's cell phone rang and he motioned the others to get up. They strolled away from the crowd and Clint followed discreetly behind.

In the parking lot, they climbed into a truck. Clint ducked behind another building as they drove past him going toward the edge of town.

He called Kurt.

"They're on the move," he told his friend.

"My three just left also. They didn't touch the fence, merely took pictures of the compound from outside. Not much they could have seen with the trees blocking the house," Kurt informed him.

"Huh." Clint didn't get what that would accomplish. Wouldn't that have been their first move? What the fuck was going on?

"I sent one of the younger guards in wolf form to see if he can follow them. Hopefully they'll stay away from town and he can see where they are meeting up," Kurt added.

"I'll head back to the compound then," Clint told him. "Hey, what were Austin and Tony doing in town?"

"Tony?" Kurt questioned. "I can see Austin chancing going in town—his Pack didn't go public so no one would recognize him—but everyone knows Tony's face."

"That's what I was thinking," Clint agreed. "Still, no one reacted to him."

"Well, we'll find out. But right now the Council is in meetings. So why don't you head over to Sara's and check on her?" Kurt suggested.

Clint wanted to see Sara and that sounded like a damn good idea. It was still early evening and she had been up later than normal with him the night before.

"You know what?" he said to Kurt. "I'm gonna do that. Call me if you need anything, though."

"Will do, man," Kurt responded. "But get some rest. Tomorrow, if they don't make a move on us, we'll force their hand. We need to end this shit and get these people out of here."

Clint couldn't agree more. They exchanged goodbyes and Clint pocketed his phone and walked toward his truck where it was parked close to Sara's shop's alley.

He knew the way to her house now with no problem. Just like the night before when he'd shown up in wolf form, he parked a block away. This time he stayed in human form and snuck around the back of Sara's property. He was almost to the edge of her yard when he heard the low command to stop. *Nice!* He was proud of the guard.

The cocking of a gun was loud next to his ear.

He raised his hands and turned to the guard. "Hey, Ryan."

Ryan Bishop was one of the full-time guards at the compound. Clint and Ryan had become fast friends and he enjoyed working with him. Ryan dropped his gun and grinned. Clint had a feeling the other man had known that it had been him he'd pulled his gun on. In fact, Ryan had probably been waiting for the opportunity. They shook hands.

"Everything cool here?" Clint asked.

Ryan nodded. "Sara and Cecil have been inside all day. I think they've been watching movies or something. They haven't even tried to go outside and no one's come close to the house, although a deputy car passes by every hour."

It didn't surprise him that Sara's dad would also send out a patrol to watch over his daughter. He slapped Ryan on the back. "Well, thanks, man. I appreciate you giving your time to watch over them."

"I didn't mind," Ryan assured him. "I've lived here a long time. I like those two."

Clint picked up a little unease from Ryan. "You okay, man?"

Ryan nodded. "Yeah. Yeah, man, I just..." Ryan blushed and looked away. "The kid? Cecil? He's..."

Clint waited.

Ryan shuffled his feet. "I've tried to talk to him a couple times. He's real shy. Young, you know, only twenty. I was worried about him, that's all."

Clint understood. Oh, boy, did he understand. "It's okay if you're interested in him. He's a good guy."

Ryan shrugged. "Yeah, I know. He's still a good six years younger than me and I don't want to make him uncomfortable, or anything."

Clint smiled at his friend. "Six years isn't much. Why don't you ask him out?"

"I couldn't… I was going…" Ryan trailed off. "Don't worry about it, man. I'm glad I could make sure he and Sara were safe."

Clint would let it go for now, but he hoped Ryan would make a move on Cecil…if Cecil wanted him to. Maybe he could drop some hints of his own.

He motioned to the house. "You can head out. I'll be here unless something else happens."

"I don't mind sticking around for a little bit," Ryan told him.

Clint nodded. He hadn't expected another answer from Ryan. "Sounds good. Give me a holler if you have any problems out here."

He walked away with a half salute to Ryan and pushed open the gate. All was quiet as he strolled up to the back door. He knocked and when Sara came into view, he waved.

She smiled. Such a beautiful welcome. Sara hurried to the door and turned the deadbolt to let him in.

He wrapped his arms around her waist and pulled her close. Their lips met and he kissed her with all the passion he felt. She moaned and he settled her against his chest as he slowed down his lips.

Aware that Ryan could probably see them, he backed off and looked down at her.

"Everything okay here?" he asked her.

She nodded. "Yeah." She ran her hands over his chest. "Cecil and I spent the afternoon watching movies. I was about to start dinner. Can you stay a little while?"

"Yes, I'll be hanging around if you think you can stand it," he teased.

She slid her hand down his stomach to cup his erection. He couldn't stop the thrust up into her hold.

"I think I can more than stand it," she assured him.

The wicked look in her eye almost burst his tight control. Knowing Ryan was outside and Cecil was just in the other room was the only thing that stopped him lifting Sara onto the counter and having his way with her. He cleared his throat and stepped back. She laughed, a soft, musical sound that made his cock twitch where it was trapped in his jeans.

"Bad girl," he kidded.

"Oh, I'll show you later how bad of a girl I can be," she promised.

Clint dropped his head back and groaned. "Trying to kill me."

Sara shook her head and scooted around behind the kitchen counter. She pulled out a pan before turning to the fridge. "Chicken okay?"

Clint nodded. "Sounds great."

She grabbed a bottle of beer and waved it at him.

He made a *give me* motion with his hand and she passed it over to him.

"Is it safe to come inside?" Cecil called from the other room.

Clint smirked at Sara as she blushed. "Yeah!" he hollered back at the younger man.

Cecil stepped into the kitchen. "I really can go home," he said once he was close by. "I'm sure no one will try anything. I don't want to be in the way."

Sara raised the knife she was using to cut the chicken into cubes. "You are not in the way! And you are staying the night."

Cecil's shoulders dropped and he nodded. Clint glanced out of the kitchen window and wondered if Ryan was watching the boy.

"She's right, man. We don't know what these people are capable of and we'd feel better having you safe and secure for the night," Clint assured Cecil.

"If you're sure," Cecil replied and sat on a stool next to Clint.

Sara set a can of Coke down in front of him.

"Besides, I'd like to get to know you, too," Clint said. He took a long pull of his brew and smiled.

"Me?" Cecil asked, surprised.

Clint nodded. "Yeah, man. You're like Sara's family, so we have to get to know each other."

Cecil beamed, clearly pleased.

"So, tell me about school," Clint requested.

While Sara cooked, Cecil started talking about the courses he was taking at the local community college. It was nice, the sounds and smells of the kitchen in the background while he sipped on a beer and talked with a very interesting man. Sara moved gracefully about the kitchen, adding a few comments to the conversation but mainly letting the two men talk. He looked up and caught her eye, and Clint knew he was in love. Sara was what he had been searching for without even knowing he was looking. She fit with him. She must have seen something in his expression, because she moved around the counter and cupped his face to give him a sweet kiss before going back to her cooking.

Cecil was grinning at him when he glanced over.

"It's so good to see her so happy. She always takes care of everyone and..." Cecil paused and shrugged. "Just thanks. Thanks for making her happy."

Clint patted Cecil on his back. "What about you?"

"What about me?"

"Anyone caught your eye?" Clint hadn't planned on asking so soon, but the subject had been brought up.

Cecil stiffened and bit his lip.

Sara stilled with her back to them.

"I... I'm not..." Cecil dropped his head.

Sara turned around and Clint frowned.

"I'm gay," Cecil confessed in a low whisper.

Well, Clint had hoped that Cecil was since he was pretty damn sure Ryan was interested.

"So, are you seeing anyone?" Clint asked again. "Got your eye on someone, maybe?"

Cecil looked up with an expression of shock. Clint smiled and dipped his head to show he wanted an answer.

Cecil shook his head. "No, no one here would..."

Clint shrugged. "You never know. You might want to keep your eyes open, just in case."

Sara had her lips pressed together and was watching him. He winked and her lips twitched. She'd understood what he meant.

"You don't mind?" Cecil's next question caught him off guard.

"That you're gay?" Clint clarified.

Cecil's head bobbed.

"Nah, man," Clint said. He hoped Cecil would relax again. He hadn't meant to cause him any stress. He had figured the kid had been out. "Got a couple friends in relationships with men. In fact, Kurt's brother is newly mated to his partner. Know a lot of damn good men that like other men."

Cecil licked his bottom lip nervously but smiled. "Cool."

Sara returned to her stove and turned off the burner. She took out plates from the cabinet and pointed to the kitchen table.

"It's ready," she declared.

Cecil jumped up and started to grab silverware and napkins while Sara filled plates. Within a couple of minutes, they were all seated at the table with plates full of chicken, pasta and vegetables.

Dinner conversation was light. They talked about the town and the winter festival that would take place next month. As Sara and Cecil described the different attractions, Clint looked forward to seeing them again. He'd attended a few when he was a young boy, but from the sound of it, the festival had grown a lot over the years. Clint would make sure that he took Sara so they could experience the festival together.

Once they'd finished one of the best chicken dishes Clint had ever tasted, Cecil jumped up and gathered the plates.

"I'll clean up!" he said. "Why don't you two go relax? I'm going to take a shower and I have some studying to do in the guest room."

Sara rose and kissed his cheek. "Thanks, hon."

Clint trailed after her and they settled onto the couch. Unlike the night before, the fire was lit. Clint settled back against the corner of the couch and pulled Sara into his arms. She lifted her head and they kissed. Soft and sweet since there was someone else in the house, but he was hyper-aware of what would happen once Cecil called it a night. Sara must have felt the same thing since she was whispering very suggestive comments in his ear as she kissed his neck.

Clint's hands shook and his cock pulsed painfully. He wanted to be inside her.

As soon as Cecil called goodnight, Sara turned to Clint and straddled his lap. "I've been waiting for this all day."

He moaned and dropped his head back when she rocked against him.

"I want to taste you tonight," she said, trailing her hands up and down his chest.

His shirt bunched under her hands and together they removed the garment.

She traveled lower, licking and tasting his skin. She lapped at the tattoo over his heart while undoing his pants. Kneeling between his legs, she tugged his jeans down and he lifted enough to have her get them off. He shivered when she lowered her head and licked the pre-cum from the tip of his cock.

"Oh, yeah," he moaned.

She looked up, gaze locked with his and oh-so slowly engulfed him.

He hissed, the feeling amazing. "Please," he actually whined.

She hummed while sucking him down. She bobbed her head, played with his balls and had gasps escaping from his throat.

Clint had to fist his hands to keep from grabbing her head and start fucking her mouth. *Damn, this may be the shortest blowjob in all of history.*

Just a touch of her tongue at the bottom of his cockhead and he forgot all pretense of control. He buried his fingers in her hair and plunged into her. He had enough sense to not force his entire length inside. Sara wasn't complaining, though. She encouraged him with her hands on his hips and tilted her head back to take more.

He howled his completion, not able to tone down the sound.

Sara rocked back on her heels, grinning. "I could do that every night."

Clint planted a hand on his chest, feeling his heart beating hard enough to worry it might burst through his chest. He didn't think he would survive that every night.

She laughed and he couldn't have that. He pushed forward and followed her down onto the floor until she was sprawled on her back with him on top.

"Your turn," he said and started yanking at her clothes. "Although next time, we really need to try to make it to your room first."

"Need you now," she demanded, pulling his head down.

They wrestled until they were both naked and wrapped around each other.

He pushed inside and took her hard and fast right there in the middle of the living-room floor. His knees ached and there would be rug burns the next day, but damn, Sara was hot.

She pushed back against him each time he slammed inside. "Harder — ride me."

What man could ever resist those words? Not him, that was for sure.

Clint wasn't proud of the fact he was too damn obsessed with her to have even taken her to bed. Eventually, they were going to have to do this on a mattress.

"Clint!" she called out to him as she climaxed.

He slowed down. Now that he'd brought her pleasure, he could think again. The passionate fog that had clouded his mind lifted and he was back in control. He gripped her hips hard before thrusting gently.

Sara was shaking, almost exhausted. He plunged half a dozen more times then came.

They collapsed down on the rug together. Sara laughed. "I hope no one was watching. Or we just gave one hell of a show."

Clint groaned. "Fuck! I forgot Ryan was outside."

She stilled. "What?"

"One of the guards is watching your house. I told him he could go back to the compound, but he said he'd stick around for a little bit. So he might not still be here."

"Oh, Jeez," she muttered.

"He'd have made himself scarce once we started."

"Or gotten off on it. Some people like to watch," she said. Her face was red with a blush, but she was smiling.

"I don't think we're his type. He wasn't here because he was ordered."

Sara sat up. "Ryan?" she asked. "I think he comes into the shop."

"Yes," he said. "Yes, he does."

"And when he does, he watches Cecil," Sara said.

"Does he?"

She laughed. "Awesome."

Clint agreed. Other than the fucking church Dan Carter had started, things were pretty damn awesome! He had to make sure they stayed that way. Perry Costa was going to get the hell out of his town.

Chapter Six

Clint looked between Austin and Tony and laughed. "That...that was a good test."

He couldn't believe he hadn't figured it out for himself. Of course, if the Church members had been just protesting the shifters, they would have been paying attention to what the shifters were doing.

Not just one, but several of them would have recognized Tony.

"So what does it mean?" he asked.

"The protesters — we feel like they're only here as a distraction. If we are worried about them, then we might let our guard down around here. Spread us thin so we don't have the same security," Gage answered. "The protesters are pawns being used by Dan Carter and Perry Costa."

"They could also be used as insurance that we won't attack while there are so many residents around, along with the media. We have to keep in mind that they think we're animals. Dan Carter has gone on record stating that we're not as smart as humans," Kurt said.

Clint snorted. "He's the one acting dumb. His entire outlook is ridiculous."

"They're baiting us, assuming we'll respond like the monsters we are," Kurt said.

"But this also puts them in no position to attack us," Clint said. "Isn't that good?"

"Unless they provoke us and can show they attacked in self-defense," Gage responded. "Most of the guards are old enough to control their tempers, but we have no idea how hard their push. We need to make sure that no one reacts."

"What if it's more than that?" Clint asked. "They want us to a retreat into the compound so they can take us all down at once?"

Tony shook his head. "Colt doesn't think so. Perry Costa is not making a move against the compound. He wants you two."

Clint exchanged a look with Kurt. "Because of what happened before? In Riverwood?"

Kurt shook his head. "I just don't know."

They sat for a few minutes, contemplating it, before Gage spoke up, "So, do we wait for them or do we force their hand?"

Without pause, both Clint and Kurt answered together, "Force their hand."

The other men nodded.

Clint was glad the Alphas agreed. He wasn't used to sitting around waiting for someone else to make a move. He wanted to get the ball rolling. He was tired of Carter, Perry and the other humans thinking they could threaten and push shifters around.

It wasn't like the shifters were out to get them. Everything had been worked out months ago. Tony and the Council had worked hard to set up open communications to assure humans there was no threat.

It took a little longer than Clint would have liked to come up with an outline that everyone agreed on. He didn't like Kurt being the target, though. It had always been his job to take care of his best friend. Putting Kurt in danger went against every bit of training he had. Clint had argued until he was red in the face. Eventually everyone else overruled him.

He was absolutely not pouting.

"Come on, man." Kurt slapped his shoulder as they changed into their jogging gear. "It makes sense. By going after me, they have fewer complications."

Clint knew that — really, he did — but it bothered him.

They stretched their muscles in preparation for their run inside the gate to the compound before nodding at the guards on duty and the plan went into play. Clint and Kurt would jog into town like before. They hadn't kept with their schedule over the last few days, but they would act like things were back to normal. Once inside the coffee shop, they would split up. Clint would pretend he was staying around with Sara, and Kurt would head back toward the compound alone.

That would give anyone watching the chance to intercept Kurt and hopefully try to take him.

The other members of the team were already spread out through town and within the woods. Kurt had also called Sheriff Webb, and the sheriff and his deputies would be keeping an eye out. If all went as planned, then Kurt would be taken. Clint, who would duck out of the back of the coffee shop, would stay on his tail while Kurt tried to find out why they wanted the two shifters. He would also do his best to ferret out any information about Dan Carter.

Tony should be contacting Colt first thing. Colt would not step in unless Kurt's life was in danger. It was still important to keep him undercover as long as possible.

Clint had run every way this mission could go over and over in his mind while they jogged. One good thing about the plan they'd decided on was that it would keep Sara out of danger. When they reached the street where most of the stores were, they found the protesters were still out in full force. News vans and reporters were scattered around.

When the first of the crowd spotted them, the mob started to yell. Insults followed the two of them while they made their way through the packed streets. Cameras turned toward them as the crowd got louder, but Clint did his best to ignore everything around him.

No one touched them, so that was a relief. But the slurs used against them were full of hatred. Clint was shocked that these so-called religious people could be so terrible, and in front of the viewers of the news stations. He'd never before come across the disgusting behavior these people were showing. He hoped the reporters were getting all of it. Kurt glanced over at him and Clint could see the same aversion on his friend's face. They slowed to a walk a few doors down from the coffee shop. Ignoring everyone around them, they stepped inside acting like they weren't bothered.

Clint was relieved to see Sara smiling behind the counter. She made the aggression toward them outside slip away. Even the tension about putting Kurt in danger eased up some. Cecil was working the machine and he looked comfortable and in his element. After this was over, he'd find a way to get Cecil and Ryan together. It wasn't normal for him to play matchmaker, but Clint was feeling the love and wanted to share the feeling.

The shop was only about half full and Clint recognized the town residents were back. He didn't spot any strangers. Good, Sara shouldn't have to deal with anger and hateful people. He was also pleased to see that the locals weren't giving the protesters the ability to take their town from them.

"Hey," he greeted Sara when he reached her. "Business looks good."

Sara laughed. "It's great. Everyone has come in this morning and said that they weren't going to let these people chase them away. This is our home and we support all our residents, fully human or not. Over a dozen people have given interviews to the reporters, stating that the entire town supports the shifters. It should be interesting to watch later."

Sara's pride in her town and friends made his heart warm.

"Good. Hopefully they won't have to deal with this for long."

Cecil set two cups of coffee down and Sara pushed them toward him and Kurt. They settled at the closest table.

So far so good. The commotion they'd caused making their way to the shop had been enough that if the men from the day before hadn't known where they were before, it was a good chance they did now.

Clint scanned the shop and noticed anytime his gaze landed on someone there, they smiled at him. He nodded back to them. It was a little weird. The residents had always been kind, and now it was like they were making a statement. Letting him know he was welcome and wanted there.

Sara finished serving an older couple, and she and Cecil joined him and Kurt at the table.

"Word has gotten around about you and Sara," Cecil told him. "They're trying to show you both that they support your relationship."

"Really?" he asked.

Cecil shrugged. "It's weird, yeah, but they mean well."

Kurt chuckled beside him, and Clint glared at his buddy. It was very cool.

"Small towns, what're you gonna do?" Sara grinned at him and he winked. Yeah, he could sure get used to this place. Sara laughed.

The four of them made small talk while Clint and Kurt finished their drinks. It was just to pass the time, but Clint still enjoyed it. He liked how Cecil preened under their attention. It was obvious the young man craved positive notice. It was sad. Clint didn't know his story, but Sara doted on him. Clint would have to find a way to help.

Fifteen minutes later, Kurt glanced at his watch and nodded. It was almost showtime. Sara must have picked up on something, because she sent Cecil to go clean some tables and leaned close to Clint.

"Be careful," she told him.

He met her lips with his for a peck. "Always am. Don't worry. I'll be by your house tonight for dinner."

She raised an eyebrow.

He mirrored the movement. It might have been better to ask, but Clint had noticed that she liked his dominant side a lot.

She laughed and waved him off. "You two get out of here. I've got work to do."

Kurt stood and stretched his arms. "I'm going back to the house," he said. "I'll catch you later, man."

Clint nodded and didn't watch him leave. Instead he kept his gaze on Sara. Sara frowned and opened her mouth, but he shook his head. It was better to not discuss the plan. Even though only locals were present, they couldn't take a chance of being overheard. Shifters did have really good hearing.

She nodded and picked up a towel before going back to work. He waited until everyone's attention was elsewhere before he slipped behind the counter.

He squeezed Sara's hand as he passed.

The rear door opened silently as he pushed it open. He glanced over his shoulder and saw Sara in the hall.

"Lock this door behind me," he ordered.

She nodded. "I don't know what you're up to, but please be careful."

"I promise." He stepped out and closed the door firmly. He started down the alley but froze when he heard a sound behind him. Clint turned slowly and relaxed as he saw Deputy Gibson. He'd met the young man a few times and he was a nice kid.

"Hey, man," Clint greeted. He knew the sheriff had his men watching out for them, but he didn't know why the deputy would be in the alley.

"Clint," Bobby Gibson said and then lifted his service weapon.

Clint took a step back right as his hearing picked up more sound behind him.

He managed to slip his phone out of his pocket. He held it to his side, hoping to be able to press Kurt's number.

He could shift, but the amount of time that it would take would leave him vulnerable. And he didn't want to get shot.

"Hey, Bobby," he spoke to the deputy but tried to see who was coming up behind him by shifting his stance. "What's this about?"

"Don't move," Gibson demanded. "They don't want you dead."

"Then what do they want?" he snapped.

If Gibson answered, he didn't hear it. Something struck the back of his head and he was falling.

He hit the ground and rolled as a boot came down on him.

* * * *

Sara grabbed the trash bags while still singing under her breath. It had been a good day at the shop and after two nights with Clint, she couldn't remember being so happy. Sara had dated in the past, although her longest relationship hadn't lasted a year. If she was being honest, she'd never even been in love. Lust? Yes. Had strong feelings? Sure. She'd never experienced the overwhelming need to be around someone. Not like she felt with Clint.

Her first thought in the morning was of Clint. The last thing she pictured was the smile on his face. She loved to see Clint smile.

His promise that he would be at her house again for dinner gave her something to look forward to. She needed to find out what his favorites foods were. She always enjoyed cooking, but making a meal for one sucked. Now she had Clint and Cecil she could cook for. She'd convinced Cecil to once again stay with her.

He'd tried to argue, but Sara was certain he was relieved she'd insisted.

Until the men that were threatening them were either gone or captured, she didn't want to chance them going after her friend.

She pushed the back door open and headed straight to the dumpster. She threw the two bags inside and did a little dance. She laughed at herself. With everything going on, she probably shouldn't have been so happy, but she couldn't help it.

After being alone so long she was enjoying the time spent with Clint. Clint had been offered a job so maybe he would be around a lot more.

He could be the man she settled down with.

She turned to head into the shop when something caught her eye.

Sara squinted and tried to make out what was on the ground but couldn't get a good look.

Cautiously, she stepped closer.

A cell phone.

And dried blood.

Oh, no! No, no, no. The only person who had been in the alley lately was Clint.

Sara dropped to her knees and grabbed the phone. It couldn't be Clint's! She began pressing buttons and looked at the outgoing calls and was horrified when she saw her own number.

"Oh, God!"

There were several missed calls and when she saw Kurt's name, she pushed the Redial button.

"Hey, man, I was getting worried," Kurt said when he answered.

"Kurt!" she cried into the phone.

"Sara?"

"Kurt! Clint's..." She didn't even know what to say. She shook so hard that it was difficult to even hold on to the phone. Clint was what? Gone? Missing?

"Calm down, honey," Kurt's calm voice came over the line. "Where's Clint?"

"I don't know!" she sobbed. "I came out to throw the trash away and his phone was here. There's...there's blood on the ground!" How could this happen? He promised that he'd be careful. She should have tried to talk him into staying. What if they killed him? Oh, God! Her knees went weak.

"Okay, Sara." Kurt raised his voice. "Are you listening to me?"

"Ye...yes." Kurt was still on the phone. He'd know what to do. Didn't shifters have special abilities? She'd read that somewhere, hadn't she?

"Sara!"

"Sorry." She needed to concentrate. Clint was out there alone and possibly hurt, or worse.

"I want you to go into the shop. Lock every door and don't open it for anyone other than me."

"Okay." She looked to the back door. It seemed so far away.

"Now, Sara!"

She jumped and raced to safety. She slammed the door closed and threw the dead bolt. She still had the phone to her ear.

"Good. Now go lock the front door. Do not open it until I tell you," Kurt commanded.

"All right."

"I'm on my way, sit tight."

Kurt hung up and Sara ran to the front. Cecil looked up when she stumbled into the counter. Her hip would bruise from the force she'd hit.

"What? What is it?"

"Clint," she managed. Sara couldn't believe the word she'd just said. This was like something out of a bad movie. One she didn't want to have a starring role in.

"What happened?"

She shook her head. She didn't know. Did she even want to know? He'd said he had it under control. That he would be fine. He'd even told her he would be there for dinner. Anger started to replace her fear and she straightened her shoulders and wiped her face. Okay, she had freaked out. There was plenty of time for that later. She needed to get her shit together and help Kurt. She could do this. She'd found Clint and there was no way that she was going to let him get taken from her.

She was known for her calmness in any situation. She would not fall apart. Being the sheriff's daughter had taught her a thing or two about hard times. When the Crawfords' house had burnt down, it was Sara who'd gathered the other residents to help them rebuild. After wild fires had savaged the surrounding areas, Sara had been in charge of taking care of the emergency crews. This was nothing different. Sara had to think about what to do next.

"Lock the front door. Don't open it for anyone but Kurt," she told Cecil, thankful that her voice was stronger. She pulled out her cell phone. Even though Clint's was still gripped in her other hand, she couldn't use it. What if someone called it? Or he did?

Her dad picked up on the second ring.

"Hi, honey," he greeted. "You headed home?"

"Dad." She was panting. *Fuck, calm down! Calm down!*

"What's wrong?" he demanded.

"Can you come to the shop? Now? Please."

"I'm already on my way. Are you hurt? Is Cecil?"

"No, we're okay. It's Clint. He's missing and it looks like someone took him."

"Okay. I'm parking my vehicle."

"Open the door," she whispered to Cecil.

Cecil nodded and went to the door and undid the lock. Her father stepped in, only stopping to reengage the lock.

"You okay?" he asked. "Neither one of you is hurt?"

"Yeah, I was just..." She waved her hand. "I don't know, but we don't need anyone worried about us. We need to be looking for Clint." Cecil stepped up and put his hand on her arm. She pulled him into her arms. They were both shaking.

"Okay, what can I do?" her father questioned.

She hugged Cecil tight. She could always count on her dad. Even if he hadn't been sheriff, Sara would have turned to him for anything. "Not sure. Let's see what Kurt says."

"Here." Her dad pulled out a chair. "Sit."

They sat at one of the tables by the door and waited. It was hard to sit still, but Sara was determined to remain calm. What she wanted to do was make some coffees or clean. Anything to keep her hands busy. She was still gripping Clint's phone.

Clint couldn't be gone. It wasn't fair. After all the years of the shifters living in Lovington without any trouble, it was now, when Sara was happy, that something happened.

She jumped when Clint's cell rang. "Hello?"

"Sara, it's Kurt."

"Any word?" *Oh, please, let them have found Clint.*

"I'm in the alley now checking it out. I've sent one of my men to the front door. You know Ryan Bishop?"

"Yes."

117

"He should be out front. Go ahead and have Cecil let him in."

"Cecil!" she called. "Can you let Ryan in the door?"

Her worker hurried to the front. Sara kept her gaze on the entrance in case of trouble while still listening to Kurt.

"Ryan's going to take you and Cecil back to your house and stay with you until we know more," Kurt was saying. "I don't want either of you to be alone."

"No, we'll be fine. You need everyone you've got to find Clint!" she protested.

"We know where Clint is," Kurt informed her.

"What!"

Kurt sighed. "We'd set up a plan for this. They were supposed to grab me, not Clint, but we're still working it. This works because it gives us the chance to appear to notice Clint's been taken and that we are looking for him."

"Oh." Sara wasn't sure what to say about that. They'd expected Kurt to be taken? That was not a good plan. She was going to talk to Clint about his ideas of being safe once they got him back.

"But since they did go for Clint instead of me, I want to tuck you and Cecil away."

"I understand," she assured Kurt. They didn't want to have to worry about them while following whatever plan it was they had. Even if she thought they were dumb.

She glanced over at Cecil and almost dropped the phone when she saw Ryan run a finger down Cecil's arm while talking with him. Well, that was very interesting, indeed.

"Did you hear me, Sara?" Kurt asked over the phone.

"What?" She hated to ask him to repeat himself.

"Trust me. Clint will be fine. I promise. This is what he does," Kurt assured her.

"Okay, thanks, Kurt," she said. "My dad's here. Do you need his help?"

She raised her eyes to meet her father's gaze.

"That would be great. Can you send him to the alley?" Kurt asked.

"Sure." She nodded toward the back door. He had a key so he'd be able to lock up behind himself. Sara smiled when he dropped a kiss onto her head before striding across the room. "He's heading to you."

"Great. Keep Clint's phone and I'll call you later with an update."

"Okay, bye." She hung up the phone and stood.

Cecil and Ryan looked over at her.

"Thanks for coming, Ryan," she said. Clint had told her about Ryan watching out for them before. She was happier to see him than she would have thought. She didn't like the idea of going home alone. Not with Clint missing. If something went wrong, surely the shifters would know pretty quick. Having Ryan with them might speed up word getting to her.

Did anyone even know about them? Well, Kurt and Ryan did. So that was something.

Clint had told her about coming to town when he was a kid to visit his dad. Sara didn't even know how to contact his family. She'd make a list of things she needed to ask Clint. Even though they'd been slow on getting to know each other, there hadn't been time to find out everything. She was going to fix that as soon as she had the chance.

"Sara?"

She lifted her head as Cecil gripped her hand. "What?"

"Ryan asked if we needed to make any stops before we go back to your house?" Cecil told her.

"Oh, no," she replied. "I have plenty of groceries. I can't think of anything else we might need." She glanced at Ryan. "Unless you think we need medical supplies or something. Do you?"

Ryan quickly shook his head. "No. Shifters heal fast. Plus I doubt Clint is going to be hurt. He has a reputation for being in some rough spots before. He's been in the military or working for the Council all his adult life. This won't do more than piss him off."

That made her feel better. "I knew he was in the military, but not what he did."

"He was in a special shifter unit," Ryan said. "Real secret, covert stuff. Kurt was the team leader," Ryan explained.

"So he and Kurt have worked together a long time?" she asked.

"Yes, Kurt won't let anything happen to Clint."

Of course, he wouldn't. Sara had seen for herself how close the two men were. If anyone wanted to find Clint more than her, it would be Kurt. "Good."

"So we're done here?" Ryan asked. "I'll feel better once I get you home behind a locked door."

"Let's go home then," she told them.

Kurt had brought Ryan with him so Sara drove with Ryan in the passenger seat and Cecil in the back. There were still protesters and strangers in the street. How had someone gotten to Clint with all the witnesses around?

Even though she was still angry, Sara drove with care through town. She didn't want to draw any attention to them. This wasn't about her. The shifters needed to concentrate on getting Clint back. Her dad could help, and she'd keep Cecil safe.

The drive to her house felt like it passed in a blur, though.

When she finally pulled up in front of her home, she breathed a sigh of relief.

"Give me your house key," Ryan said. He held out his hand. "I want to check the outside and in. If I'm not back in five minutes, drive straight back to the sheriff's office."

"We can't leave you!" Cecil exclaimed.

Ryan turned his head to smile at Cecil over his shoulder. "Yes, you will." He gazed at Sara.

She nodded. It would be hard, but she could get help for him if something happened. Sara worked the house key off her ring and handed it over. "Just be careful."

"Five minutes." Ryan exited the vehicle, letting in a cold gust of wind.

"I don't like this," Cecil mumbled.

Sara agreed, but didn't say anything out loud. It would all be okay. They'd have Clint back by the time dark fell. They had to. He'd promised to be there for dinner. She needed to keep the faith.

Chapter Seven

Clint's head was pounding and there was a horrible taste in his mouth. So not only had he been knocked out, but also drugged. Which meant that he had no idea how long he'd been out. It could be hours or a day, depending on how much of the drugs they used and what kind. He listened carefully without moving a muscle in order to use his senses to search for any danger around him. He was alone at the moment. The scent of humans was strong, though. Maybe they thought he'd be unconscious for a while. If Clint had enough time, he was certain he'd find a way out.

He remembered everything that had taken place. The deputy in the alley, the sound behind him and, finally, seeing two men's feet when he'd been falling. He knew he had to hold back his anger. He didn't want to alert anyone that he was awake yet. But, man, was he pissed! He should have suspected something like this. But, in all honesty, he hadn't given the humans much credit. They hadn't been acting very smart. Plus the wolves had an inside man. His guard had been down, expecting them to go after Kurt. And he'd been distracted by Sara. It was his own fault he was in this situation. He hoped the others realized he was missing. Kurt would get worried if the other men made it back to the compound and Clint didn't check in. Sara would be concerned if he didn't make it to dinner.

But the unknown was what he had a problem with. He had no way of knowing if Kurt had also been taken and he hoped like hell that Sara was safe.

Not sensing anyone around him, he blinked his eyes open. The room he was inside was practically empty. He lay on an old beaten wood floor with his hands and ankles tied together. With silver chains? Were they fucking kidding him? Silver didn't do anything to shifters. Why would it? He snorted. These idiots believed all the Hollywood movies and paranormal books. Well, good news for him. That would make escaping easier.

He rolled to his knees, fighting nausea. Probably had a concussion from the hit to the back of his head, but he could work through that. He managed to make it to his knees to sit up and bit back a groan. The windows were boarded up, but he could still see light shining through, so at least he hadn't been down for long.

Footsteps caught his attention and he braced himself for what was coming. With practiced ease, he calmed himself.

The plan is still in effect, he told himself. Kurt would know something was wrong and they already knew the most likely place he had been taken, thanks to Colt. He had to get through until he was rescued or got himself out. He also needed to find out where Dan Carter was hiding. That would be easier if it was Carter headed his way.

He waited for the door to open. Perry Costa and two other men entered.

"You're awake," Perry Costa said in greeting as the door closed behind him.

Clint remained silent. It usually drove people crazy. The more Perry talked, the better the chance of him revealing something.

"I apologize for the means we had to use to get you here, but you and your friend would not cooperate," Perry said coolly and leaned against the wall with his arms crossed.

The two other men moved around the room to stand behind him.

Clint raised a brow.

Perry frowned. "What, nothing to say? You had a pretty smart mouth last time we met. And here I've gone through all this trouble."

"Well, if I'd known the accommodations were so nice, then I would have reserved a room," Clint sniped. Fuck remaining silent. This asshole pissed him off.

Perry Costa shook his head. "Pity."

A foot to his back had Clint grunting as he tried to catch himself. His hands broke his fall and saved him from face-planting. Barely.

Clint growled as he pushed himself back up. "Not to mention the staff here is *soooo* polite," he drawled, still trying to catch his breath.

This time, the kick was to his side. He managed to avoid the worst of the blow, expecting it, but it still fucking hurt.

"We can do this all day," Perry told him.

So could Clint. He opened his mouth to taunt him further, but gasped instead when his hair was grabbed and his head was jerked back.

Perry crouched down in front of him. "Listen carefully."

Clint just glared.

"I can turn you over to the Church. They'll probably burn you at the stake or something. They really believe that you are evil and wish to get rid of each and every one of your kind," Perry informed him.

"And you don't?" Clint asked through clenched teeth.

Perry shrugged. "There is a little evil in us all, don't you think? I, however, have another reason for wanting you."

Clint couldn't wait to hear this. Perry was going off script. That was not good news. If he was going up against Carter, then Clint knew what to do, but with Perry stepping out of line, there were too many possibilities of something going wrong. But Clint's training included being able to think on his feet. Instead of going against all Carter's organization, it would be much easier taking care of Perry and his few followers.

Perry was quiet for several moments before he grinned. It was a nasty grin and Clint wanted to deck him. If only he could get his hands free.

"It's simple. You do something for me and I will avoid giving you, your partner, girlfriend and every other shifter over to the church."

"Kill you?" Clint replied with a smile of his own.

Perry laughed. "Nothing that dramatic."

Clint lifted an eyebrow.

"It's simple," Perry said. "Turn me into one of your kind, and I will let you go."

Clint gaped at the other man. "That…that's what you want?" Clint asked, shocked. It wasn't even possible! Clint started to laugh, at first low and quiet, then louder and a little more hysterical. This man was nuts.

"I'm pleased this amuses you," Perry snapped.

"You want me to turn you into a shifter," Clint repeated.

"Yes, one bite. That is all that I ask for your freedom. I even have the ability to talk to Carter and have him leave you and this town alone. He trusts me." The smugness in is tone grated on Clint's nerves. Perry honestly believed what he was saying. Perry was willing to exchange the town's freedom to become a shifter.

"You want me to bite you, and you'll leave and take all your people with you?" Clint asked, just to buy himself time to decide what to do. He wished Kurt was there. While Clint knew how to fight, hunt and protect, Kurt was much better at negotiations. Clint didn't want to say the wrong thing. But all he could think was Perry was so unhinged he was unpredictable.

"Exactly," Perry replied.

Clint shook his head. He knew that when the shifters went public, one very important point had been made over and over. Shifters could not turn a human into one of them.

You had to be born a shifter.

"Don't you know that's impossible?" Clint questioned. Even if he wanted to change Perry, he couldn't.

Perry snorted. "I know that's the position the government is taking, but we both know the truth."

Clint had to play this smart. Perry Cole wanted to be a shifter? Well, since Clint knew that wasn't even a possibility, he could have a little fun with this while he waited for his rescue. Or he could try to get free. Maybe all he needed to do was ask?

"Untie me," he demanded.

Perry gave a triumphant cry while Clint was roughly lifted to his feet. The two goons in the room with him and Perry would be something he worried about later. First, he'd need to eliminate Perry. He was released from his binding with quick jerks. Clint rolled her neck and shoulders. Wow, he'd been bound a while. He hoped Kurt and Sara weren't too worried. There was probably a pretty intense hunt for him.

"Don't try anything funny," Perry ordered, pointing his finger at Clint. Now that Clint stood in front of him, the scent of Perry's fear radiated off him.

Clint gave him his best innocent face, then smiled.

"I'm not a moron," Perry told him. "You know Deputy Gibson is involved. Right now, he has your girlfriend with him. If anything happens to me, she will disappear."

Clint jerked against the hands that still held them. Son of a bitch! He was going to kill every single one of them. Sara was never supposed to be involved in this. Clint growled.

"But that is nothing compared to what will happen to your partner. As we speak, Carter's boys are driving Kurt to Dan Carter. If everything goes as planned, I'll call them back. If not..." Perry shrugged. "He'll be delivered to Carter and his men."

"And where exactly is that?" Clint questioned. He hoped Perry kept talking. He'd stall as long as he could.

"Not something you need to worry about."

"What happens after I bite you?" Clint asked.

"I'll have all your friends released. I'm a man of my word. Plus we'll be on the same side."

"Same side?" Clint snorted.

"Yes." Perry laughed. "We're all aware that the ultimate goal for the shifters is to be in charge. You want to rule. So do I. I'm not going to be one of the human cattle after the takeover."

Wow, Perry's imagination was going wild. If the shifters had wanted to take control of the world, they'd have already done it. For sure, they wouldn't have announced their presence to ensure humans felt safe around them. All the shifters wanted was to be able to live their lives. Stricter hunting laws so, when in their animal forms, they didn't have to worry about getting shot.

The hands holding him tightened. "What about your men here?" Where the two goons going to allow Clint to bite Perry and not do anything about it? Wasn't there loyalty in the church?

"You don't get to bite them," Perry said. "I don't want them part of your Pack. They will belong to me. After you show me what I need to know, I'll make them like us. They'll be the first."

"You plan on making your own Pack?" Clint asked.

"Of my chosen."

"What about Dan Carter?" Surely, Carter didn't have anything to do with this.

Perry shrugged. "Carter doesn't understand the way the world is changing. He wants to get rid of each and every one of you. I see a better future for us. I'll take care of Carter if he becomes a problem to me and my Pack."

Perry was already talking like this was a done deal. Clint wasn't sure where he should go from here. If he bit Perry and the man wasn't turned into a shifter, they would all be killed. If he killed Perry, then that put Sara and Kurt in danger.

"So what's it gonna be?" Perry asked. "Are you going to change me and save the people you care about? It's not like I plan to tell anyone other than my trusted few. The secret will be safe with me."

He had to take the chance. Had to trust Kurt and the Alphas to stick with the plan and have everything handled. He hated to have to depend on them, but with Sara in danger, he had no choice.

Because no matter what Perry Costa wanted, Clint was not able to turn him into a shifter.

Clint nodded.

Perry motioned to the other two men and he was released. Then he was jabbed by the cold metal barrel of a gun.

"Just in case you're thinking about doing anything stupid," Perry told him.

Clint stretched to his full height and was pleased when Perry took a step back. He knew his bulk was intimating and he planned on using everything in his arsenal.

"I'll need to shift," Clint told him. "I don't want to get shot in the middle of it."

Perry backed up against the wall once again. Clint angled his body so he could keep all three men in his eye line. Shifting would put him in a dangerous position while transforming, but he had to trust his instincts. And he believed they wouldn't attack him as he shifted.

Perry Costa wanted something from him.

Clint started to remove his clothes, not tearing his gaze from the others. The men with him didn't even have the decency to look away. They just stared back. How rude.

Clint shook his head, crouched and started the transformation.

Within moments, he was shaking off the change and faced the three men as a large wolf. In his wolf form, all of his senses were sharper and the smell of fear filled the room.

The two men with Perry were terrified. Perry himself was visibly shaking.

That was good. He could play with that.

Clint took his time to stretch, knowing he was adding to the men's terror. He opened his mouth wide, making sure they got a good look at his sharp teeth.

"He's big," the redhead said. Out of the three humans, he was the one fighting his fight-or-flight instinct. Deep down, the huge man was a coward.

"I knew I chose right," Perry stated. "He is going to make us so powerful. Keep the faith, my friends."

But Perry was in this alone. He was the one who Clint needed to take out.

When he was ready, he stalked toward Perry.

The man didn't look so sure now that he was faced with the animal. Perry held up a hand and spoke slowly. "Just one bite. If you attack me, my men will shoot you and Kurt and Sara will also suffer."

If Clint could smile in this form, he would have. He kept heading toward his prey. His wolf nature was strong and all he wanted to do was rip out the throats of the three humans before finding Kurt and Sara. Perry was correct in his statement that Clint was powerful.

He stopped right in front of Perry. He heard the cock of the gun behind him and turned his head. The other two men had stepped close to each other and one of them still held a gun on him.

Clint wasn't worried. Not only was he faster in this form, but the man's hand was shaking so badly Clint didn't think he could hit anything he was aiming for.

He turned his attention back to Perry and eyed him.

He didn't plan on killing the man. Not really. Even if he wanted to tear the flesh from Perry's body. That wasn't his job. Oh, he would if it came down to it, but really, Perry and his men needed to be taken and arrested.

Clint lunged for Perry's arm and bit down hard.

Perry screamed. The sound echoed in the small room.

* * * *

The bedroom still smelled of Clint. Sara sat on her mattress and ran her hand over the comforter. It hadn't been that long since she'd woken up with Clint's arms around her.

Would she ever in his embrace again? How long could he be held without receiving serious injuries? She'd been tempted to pull out her laptop and do more research on shifters, but she was afraid of what she'd find. Maybe not knowing was better.

With a sigh, she stood. Cecil and Ryan had gone into the kitchen and she needed to take care of her guests. She strolled out of the room, resisting the urge to look back. The later it got, the more she doubted that Clint would be back in her bed. It hurt. More than Sara had though possible. How had Clint worked his way so deep in her heart already?

She was a sensible woman who had been on her own long enough to know how the world worked. Clint hadn't even committed himself to her. Sure, he'd said he'd gotten a job offer to stay, but he'd never told her that he'd accepted. If he was found, that didn't mean there was a future between them. But, God, she ached for one.

If she could have handpicked the perfect man for her, it would be Clint.

She had too much to think about. First thing she needed to worry about was if Clint even made it back. Until she knew he was safe, everything else could wait.

Sara walked into the kitchen and stopped short when she spotted Cecil in Ryan's arms. The two men were locked together in a passionate kiss, so she tried to back out in silence. Cecil moaned and wrapped his arms around the older man's shoulders while grinding against him.

Holy shit!

She must have made a sound, because Ryan pulled his mouth away from Cecil's while keeping hold of him.

Ryan glanced over at her and grinned.

Sara knew her mouth was hanging open, but that scene had been unexpected. She knew Cecil had casually dated a few guys he'd met at school, but with Cecil being so shy, it made it hard for him to get close to anyone.

Ryan started to chuckle while Cecil buried his head against his chest.

Sara rocked back on her heels and grinned. "Sorry, I didn't mean to interrupt anything."

Cecil pulled away from Ryan, blushing, and offered a small smile of his own.

Sara was very happy for her friend. She'd suspected for a while that Ryan had a crush on Cecil and was thrilled he was finally making his move. It had certainly taken him long enough.

Ryan was one of the first shifters who had come into her coffee shop on a regular basis. Every time he was there, he tried to engage Cecil in conversation.

She'd wanted to encourage Cecil but had decided to let them work out their feelings by themselves. Now she was glad she had.

"Coffee?" Cecil asked, hurrying around the counter.

He was obviously embarrassed and she winked at Ryan before strolling to the counter. She wouldn't tease Cecil. This time, anyway.

"That would be great," she answered instead as she sat on one of the stools.

"Ryan?"

"Yeah, thanks."

Cecil flushed and turned away to mess with the espresso machine. "How about lattes?"

"Perfect," Sara praised.

He began grinding the beans as Ryan's cell phone rang. Ryan stepped away and Sara was able to watch Cecil. She didn't want to think about who could be on the other end of the phone. She figured if it had been Clint, then Ryan would have stayed. So he would keep her attention on Cecil until she knew for sure. Her friend might be shy, but he was obviously very pleased with Ryan's attention. He had a spring in his step as he worked.

He peeked up at her. She grinned in return. "What?" he asked.

"Nothing," she replied. "Nothing at all."

He huffed before putting his hands on his hips. "Just get it out of your system."

"Really." She held her hands up. "I'm not saying anything. Not about your well-kissed lips or the beard burn on your neck." Okay, it was not her fault that Cecil was so easy to tease.

Cecil groaned.

"It was a compliment," she said.

Ryan came back to the counter and Sara glanced over at him. The tension on his face was obvious. So it hadn't been a good call, as she'd suspected. Sara gripped her knees to keep her hands steady.

"What's wrong?" she whispered. "Is it Clint? Was he hurt?" Please, please, don't let him have been killed.

Ryan paled. "No."

He breathed out a long sigh. "Okay."

"They are having trouble finding him at all. He's not at the location we thought he'd be taken to," Ryan told them.

Sara gripped the counter hard. "What's that mean?" she asked although she knew. They had no idea where Clint was. Or what he was going through. All kinds of horrible images flashed in her mind. *Torture. Death. Holy shit, Clint…*

"It's okay." Ryan placed his hand on her shoulder. "We have help in locating Clint. And he's one of the strongest wolves I have ever known."

"Yeah, but…" *Oh, God!* She couldn't even say the words.

"I haven't been in on all the planning," Ryan said. "But there have been a lot of visitors in the past few days. All of them are well-known strong shifters."

"That doesn't help Clint," she exclaimed. "He was the one taken, not them."

"True, but these are the men we want out there," Ryan said. "They'll find him."

"It's been hours," she said. Sara rubbed her chest where an ache had bloomed.

"That was Kurt," Ryan said. "Some friends arrived and with them a tracker. The best tracker out there. They're about to shift and search. They've narrowed it down to three locations."

Sara bobbed her head. She could hear the words that Ryan was saying, but she couldn't get the pictures out of her mind that Clint was lying somewhere hurt or worse.

"Sara? Did you hear me?" Ryan asked. Cecil came around the counter to put his arm over her shoulder.

"What?"

Ryan smiled. "I'm going to tell you a secret, but you can't let anyone else know. Either of you."

"Okay." She agreed. Sara would agree to anything.

"We have an inside man with the group that took Clint."

She gasped.

"One call from this guy and we'll know where Clint is. He'll also step in if Clint's life is in danger."

"But so much can go wrong. Has gone wrong," Sara said.

"They know what they're doing," Ryan tried to assure her. "This is what they do."

Sara nodded. Ryan had faith in his friends. Clint believed in the men to have his back. Was it too much to ask that Sara did, too? Although she'd throw some prayers in there, as well.

"Let me finish the drinks," Cecil said. "Something hot will help."

"Yeah, okay."

"Trust me — Kurt will find Clint." Ryan reached over and grasped her hand. "I haven't known them long, but I knew of them."

"Really?" She clung to the change of subject.

Ryan laughed. "They've been working for the Council of Alphas for years."

"Council?" she asked.

"Do you know any other shifters?" Ryan asked.

Cecil set a vanilla latte in front of her and Sara wrapped her hands around her mug. Cecil leaned against her side. They both shook their heads.

"This place is special," Ryan said. "And I'm only telling you two this because I know how Clint feels about you, Sara." He gazed at Cecil. "It's the same way I do about that man by your side."

Cecil beamed back at him. Sara had to laugh. Even in the middle of her worry. Ryan was smooth.

"Anyway." Ryan cleared his throat. "This isn't a typical Pack of shifters."

Sara had often thought that the secrecy, even after the shifters had announced their presence was weird.

"The shifters who live at the compound are all Alphas," Ryan said.

"I thought Alphas led Packs," she said.

"Normally, they do. Except these Alphas have given up their Packs and hold seats on the Council. As the Council, they advise and watch over all of the Packs."

She sipped the rich, strong espresso brew. Sara thought she understood.

"Other Alphas can contact the Council to request help. A few weeks ago, the Alpha from Riverwood contacted the Council after a series of fires."

"Clint told me about that. And I saw some of it on the news," Sara said. Cecil nodded.

"Kurt is from that Pack, so of course, it was the two of them who volunteered to go. I think the Council had six or seven teams that work like Kurt and Clint. Traveling from Pack to Pack and helping where they can."

"It's so organized," Cecil commented.

"We wouldn't have been able to stay hidden for so long without being well-prepared," Ryan said.

"True," Sara agreed. "So Kurt and Clint go around the country helping people?"

"Yes," Ryan said. "A few years ago, there was someone attacking female wolf shifters. The Pack of these women banded together to try to figure out who was responsible. Kurt and Clint were sent by the Council to assist."

"Wow," Cecil murmured. "They're real heroes."

Sara thought the same.

"Another time, the feline shifter Prince was kidnapped. The Prince's family didn't want him to side with the wolf shifters and come out in the open. The Council sent out numerous teams to try to find him."

"Was he found?" Sara asked. "I think I've seen him on the television."

"Yes," Ryan said. "The Prince was rescued by his own mate and another team. But Kurt and Clint spent months searching."

So Clint would be giving up his whole life to stay in Lovington. Sara hadn't thought about what he did before coming to town.

"But they're based out of here," Ryan said. "So they visit often." Ryan sent her a look that said he knew what she was thinking. "Plus I've been told that they've been offered job that would keep them in the compound."

"Clint told me that," she confessed.

"This is the longest they've ever stayed at one time. I think they like it. A wolf shifter isn't meant to travel so much. We need Pack and home. This offer will allow both of them to settle down."

If that was what they wanted. Clint might not be ready to stay in one place. But that didn't mean that he didn't care about Sara. Even if he had to go and help other Packs, he'd always come back.

Something inside Sara settled.

A lot of people made long-distance relationships work and they weren't doing something as important as Clint.

If he needed to take trips in order to keep the shifters safe, she could deal with that. Sara's home was there in Lovington with her family, friends and little coffee shop. After Clint finished saving others, he'd have a place to return. A warm and welcoming home in the arms of the woman who might love him.

She might not be able to save the world, but she could offer him security, of Pack, or home. That was what she could do.

Ryan was smiling at her when she looked up.

"What?" She frowned.

"I can practically see the wheels turning in your head. All these plans you're making. Clint is a lucky guy."

"Yeah," she agreed. "He is. And I'm going to make sure he knows it." Sara stood and walked around the island. "We need food for everyone. They're out there doing what they can, so we'll do the same," she stated.

Cecil rushed over to the pantry. "What're you thinking?" he asked. "You have the ingredients for your chili. As cold as it is, I bet that would go over well."

"Great idea," she praised. She pulled the hamburger meat out of the freezer to start it defrosting.

Ryan rose. "I'm going to patrol around the house, then I'll be in to help."

"Be careful," Cecil told him.

"I will." Ryan winked at him. "I can't wait to taste this chili you're so excited about."

"It's awesome!" Cecil said.

Sara laughed. It was her grandma's recipe and perfect for a cold night. The entire kitchen would be filled with delicious scents of spices. Just what they needed as they waited on word about Clint.

Chapter Eight

Clint dropped Perry's arm and the man fell to his knees, grasping his injured limb, tears pouring down his face. Yeah, Clint had bitten him hard. He'd made damn sure that it had hurt. The man had asked for a bite and Clint had delivered. That would keep Perry out of the action for a little bit.

The other two men in the room had gone pale and Clint turned his attention to them. He made a big show of licking his mouth where he knew there would be blood.

Then he launched himself.

He knocked the dark-haired man down while he clamped his jaw on the gun hand of the other. The weapon clattered to the floor and the three of them went down. He let go of one man's hand and turned to bite the dark-haired one on the leg. He was pushed but held tight to his target.

It wasn't easy to concentrate on his prey with the blows to his side. He was glad that a shot hadn't been fired. It didn't take silver bullets or any of that kind of bullshit to kill a shifter. A regular lead bullet in the right place worked as well. Clint was taking a chance that he'd surprised the men enough that they weren't thinking clearly.

Perry was yelling, but with blood dripping from his own wound, he was unable to stand and help his men. The dark-haired human whimpered and cried from under Clint.

"No! No!" the red-headed man who had held the gun yelled. "I don't want to be a monster." He climbed to his feet and ran for the door. Clint didn't try to stop him.

Clint let go of his current opponent, who curled up in a ball. He would have snorted if he could. They were such big and bad men when they'd had Clint tied up but now look at them.

He headed toward the door that the first human had left open in his rush to get away.

Behind him, Perry was struggling to his feet while yelling at Clint.

More running footsteps sounded, coming closer, so Clint needed to hurry in order to get away. He'd gotten lucky with Perry and his two goons. Clint couldn't depend on his luck holding, though. More humans would either result in his recapture, murder or the humans getting hurt.

Clint raced through a narrow hallway, using the stench of fear the redhead had left trailing, hoping that he was nearing the front door.

Yes! He could see sunlight pouring in.

The idiot had even left the front door open. The sound behind him was getting closer. Clint had to take a chance. He sped up, his claws clicking on the old tile, then soared through the entry.

Several men yelled and scrambled from the porch as Clint hopped down the broken steps. At least six humans surrounded him. He swung his head around, looking for the best exit.

Trees surrounded the area. And several people were running his way. He threw his head back and howled. It was a warning, a call to Pack and a desperate instinct of survival.

Most of the humans stopped. Clint didn't see any weapons, either.

One brave, young man with a goatee and tattoos crept closer to Clint.

Clint snarled in return. The man froze, lifting his hands up.

From the corner of his eye, he saw more men approaching. Clint turned his head in that direction as a sheriff's truck sped around the house then slid to a stop close to him. Clint ducked low and bared his teeth, not knowing who was in the vehicle. A deputy had been involved after all. Sara! He needed to find out where she was being held.

Clint crouched, ready to pounce.

"Clint!" Kurt called to him. He jumped from the passenger side. Sheriff Webb climbed out of the driver's side of the truck. Clint sat up. Kurt was there. Holy shit! Yes! His friend was safe. But why was the sheriff there? They needed to find Sara. If word got out that Clint was rescued, then she would be in danger.

Kurt hurried over to him and dropped to his knees. "You okay?"

Clint moved his head in confirmation. He looked around at the Council guards, Gage, Tony and even

Alpha Babcock taking charge of the scene. Sheriff Webb was directing the arrest of the humans.

"We got them," Kurt confirmed. "They're all going to pay. Where's Perry?"

Clint rose and headed back toward the house.

"I got it," Austin said as he and Gage hurried past them.

"Let's get you to an area to shift," Kurt suggested and Clint followed him toward some trees.

Once they were out of sight, Clint shifted back to human form. He panted from exhaustion with everything that had taken place. Kurt stood by his side as he rested his hands on his knees and hung his head.

In just a few minutes, he would have to tell everyone what had happened. He looked up at his best friend. "You okay? Sara?"

Kurt laughed. "Yeah, man, I'm fine. Sara's waiting at her house for you."

Clint shook his head. "They said they had you and Sara."

"Nope." Kurt grinned. "Ryan and Cecil are with Sara. I spoke to them not long ago. And as you can see" — he waved his hand up and down his body — "I'm still as handsome as before."

Clint snorted and accepted Kurt's hand to help him rise. Kurt swung the backpack off his shoulder and tossed it to him. Inside he found jeans, a T-shirt, socks and shoes. He quickly dressed.

"How'd you find me?" he questioned once he was dressed and they'd started toward everyone else. Not that it was unexpected, but Clint liked to have all the information.

"Colt," Kurt explained. "Damn, that guy is good. As soon as Sara found your phone in the alley and called me, I called Tony and he got hold of Colt."

"He's here?" Clint asked. Why had he allowed Perry to get bitten?

"No," Kurt said. "It seems Perry took half of the men, the humans who seem to follow him more than Dan Carter. Colt wasn't in that group. But Colt had visited several houses that Perry had looked to and made us a list. We also called in some help."

"So, I did see RJ and Mike?" Clint asked.

The men coming from the trees right before the sheriff's vehicle had arrived had looked familiar. Hell, he'd seen them in Riverwood.

"Yep," Kurt confirmed. "After we couldn't find you at the first house, I called Alpha Nelson. RJ was still there visiting Mike and they were on the way before I even hung up the phone with the Alpha."

Clint chuckled. It was good to have friends who would drop anything and come to his rescue. "We need to keep RJ away from Perry. He'll eat him alive."

Kurt eyes shined with laughter. "I know."

"And Sara is okay?" Clint asked. He'd felt so guilty about getting her involved. Now it seemed she'd been safe the whole time.

"Yes, we'll call her in a minute. First, you need to tell me how they got you."

Shit. "I need to find the sheriff."

"Let's go," Kurt said.

"I still don't understand how Colt knew about these houses if Perry didn't trust him. Perry is acting against Dan Carter's orders."

"Colt hadn't heard anything about you being taken and nosed around," Kurt continued. "When he couldn't find anything, he cornered that guy Rudy who he'd been hanging with."

Clint nodded. Sara had been worried the man would go after Cecil.

"Colt told him if he didn't tell Colt what was going on, he'd tell everyone Rudy was gay. Said he had proof to back it up."

"What?"

"Yeah, Colt had seen him with one of the other young men of the Church and had snapped some pictures with his cell phone. He wasn't going to use them unless Rudy got out of hand, but he couldn't think of any other way to find out where you were. He doesn't want to out the man."

"Wow!" Clint exclaimed. "Guess I was lucky Colt knew how to play him."

"Yeah," Kurt agreed. "Colt says he's not such a bad guy. Or not the worst of the bunch. I guess his parents are deep in the Church and since he's been told as soon as he was able to talk that homosexuals were evil, he's scared to death someone will find out. But he's also young and horny, so it's a fine line he's walking."

"That does suck."

"Colt's going to try to help him while he's undercover. He told Rudy he wanted to know because he didn't like to be left out of things and didn't like Perry. He said Rudy seems terrified of Perry and wonders if Perry knows what Rudy's hiding and using it against him."

"Damn, this is all..." Clint waved his hand around. "They think shifters are evil, but Perry wanted me to bite him so he could become one of us. These people... I will never understand why they act this way. Does it matter if a shifter lives in town? Why is that the biggest worry anyone has?"

"Yeah, it doesn't make sense, but it's been going on for so long I don't see it changing any time soon, either," Kurt agreed. "Colt says that's not even the tip of the iceberg with these folks, though. I guess that's why he's staying in longer. He wants to help the people who don't want to be there. Wants to be able to get them out."

"Well, I'd like to help if we can," Clint told him.

"That's what I said. Colt's joining the chapter of the Church close by. That's where Rudy is stationed and Perry was supposed to head it up."

"So Dan Carter wouldn't know that Perry was a shifter and Perry could still do his bidding."

They stopped and watched as Perry and the last man came out in handcuffs.

"He bit me!" the dark-haired man was crying. "I'm going to turn all furry."

Both Kurt and Clint laughed. Perry was glaring at him.

"It's not going to work, is it?" Perry asked. He had a bandage over his arm that was already starting to bleed through.

"Nope," Clint said with a grin.

Perry shook his head and his shoulders slumped.

Sheriff Webb came out of the house and strolled over to them.

"You need to pick up Deputy Gibson, too," Clint informed him. "Before he runs."

"Bobby?"

"Yeah," Clint said. "He's the one who approached me behind Sara's shop. Perry told me he was holding her until I did what he wanted."

"Well, shit." Sheriff Webb ran his hands roughly over his face. "I trusted him. I've sent him out several times to watch over her."

"Everything okay?" Austin asked as he and Gage joined them.

"I need to do some cleaning up inside my station," Sheriff Webb stated. "I can't believe this." He stomped away. Clint felt for the man. It couldn't be easy finding people to trust. Plus if the sheriff had put Bobby Gibson in charge of Sara's safety, that would be a double blow.

Clint turned to Austin and Gage. "Thanks for the assist," he said. He hadn't wanted to kill anyone. If they'd tried to recapture him, Clint would have fought for his life.

Gage laughed. "Damn, you could have at least waited for the rescue team. I never get to have any fun anymore."

Austin slapped Gage on the back, chuckling. "I won't mention that to Marisa."

Gage mock growled and swiped his hand over the back of Austin's head. "And I won't tell Kiley had you went running in without any concern for weapons. We both know she'll kick your ass."

Everyone laughed as the stress of the day began to ease.

They might not have found Dan Carter, but they still had Colt inside. With Perry and his cronies charged with kidnapping and assault, Carter was going to have to come out of hiding or assign someone else to the area.

Everyone that Clint cared about was safe and sound. All in all, it had been a good day. He cleared his throat. "I need to —"

"Go see your woman," Kurt finished.

Clint nodded. "I need to know she's okay. See with my own eyes."

Alpha Babcock walked up. He patted Clint's shoulder. "I'm glad to hear things are going well with Sara. She's a bright girl."

Clint turned to the Council member. "You know Sara?"

Alpha Babcock grinned. "I don't sit in my office. I keep a close eye on my town. Even if they never see me."

"Of course," Clint agreed. He shouldn't be surprised. The Council had a relationship with the town folk and sheriff.

"In the morning, we'll all meet up and see what our next steps are going to be. With Colt still undercover, we have a lot more work to do. I want Dan Carter found."

Clint, Kurt and the others nodded. It wasn't finished yet, but at least the threat that Perry had posed was over. Maybe Lovington could get back to normal. Clint could go back to his morning runs and visiting Sara at the shop. At night, they could curl up in front of the fire before going to bed, which meant that he would be taking the offer the Council had made of a full-time job at the compound. He hoped Kurt would stay with him. He thought he might. They'd been through so much and Clint didn't want to lose his best friend. But when he thought about the future, it was Sara he saw, from the way her nose scrunched up when she teased Cecil to the sparkle in her eyes as she looked at Clint with passion.

He turned to Kurt and punched his best friend in the arm. "Driver! Get the car."

Kurt flipped him off but laughed. "We're parked farther up the road. Come on."

Clint followed as Kurt led the way back to his truck. It wasn't until he was surrounded by the tall trees and under the canopy of leaves that he finally breathed normally.

"So are we going to talk about it?" Kurt asked.

"What?" Clint glanced at his best friend. What was he even talking about.

"If I told you we needed to leave right now to go down to Texas, what would you say?" Kurt asked.

All the relief Clint had felt about seeing Sara fled. "Why didn't you tell me earlier?" He was disappointed, but this was his life.

"Really, man?" Kurt turned and frowned at him.

Clint stopped. "What?"

"You'd jump in the truck and leave with me?" Kurt demanded.

"Uh, yeah," Clint said. "That's my job. Our job."

"What about Sara?"

"What about her?" Clint repeated. "I want to see her, but she'll understand. I'll call her from the road." Fuck, where was his cell? "Or maybe we can stop by real quick?" He'd be happy with a quick visit.

"Jesus, man!" Kurt exclaimed. "You're in love with her."

"Yes?" Clint didn't understand what Kurt was going on about. "What the fuck is happening right now?"

"I'm trying to find out if you want to accept the positions here or if you want to continue doing what we have been."

Clint laughed. "Of course, I want to stay here." He narrowed his eyes at his best friend. "I thought you knew that."

"Well, you never said anything," Kurt replied. "And you were going to go with me."

"So we don't have to go to Texas?" Clint asked.

"No!" Kurt yelled.

"Oh, thank God!" Clint said.

Kurt made a sound in his throat as though he was being strangled.

"What?" Clint asked. "I want to see Sara, but if we were needed somewhere else, I'd have gone. But I would return to her." Clint didn't know what Kurt had been thinking.

"So you want to stay?" Kurt asked again.

"Yes." Clint eyed his best friend. "I like it here and I think we'll both be happy. We've been traveling for years. I want a home."

"Me, too," Kurt stated. "I'm getting too old for this shit."

Clint laughed. "I don't agree with that. But Sara is who I want to be with."

"Okay, let's get you to your girl then. I'll take care of getting things set up with the Council."

* * * *

Sara was on pins and needles. Ryan had gotten word that Clint had been found and all was okay, but he hadn't talked to Kurt or Clint. It was someone named Austin who'd called. Clint was supposed to be on his way to her house. All Sara could think about was what could go wrong before he arrived. She tried not to think about what Clint might have gone through. She suspected she would have to wait until the next day to see him and, while she understood, she really wanted to run her hands over him and make sure he was uninjured.

She sighed and stood. They'd retired to the living room, but she couldn't settle. She grabbed the glasses they'd used earlier.

Ryan and Cecil were curled onto the couch together, watching a movie, Cecil's head on Ryan's chest.

"Need help?" Ryan offered.

"Nah, I just...need to move."

He nodded back. "I understand."

She smiled a little as she went into the kitchen. She liked Ryan and was glad he'd finally made a move on her friend. Cecil was in heaven at the moment. She rinsed out the glasses and placed them in the dishwasher. Afterward Sara wiped down the already clean counter, her gaze traveling to the backyard. So much had changed in the last several weeks. She found herself in a world she couldn't have imagined. And Clint... She had strong feelings for Clint.

Movement outside the window caught her attention. Her breath hitched.

Clint walked slowly through the backyard toward the house.

She rushed to the door, hand already reaching to turn the dead bolt, then raced to him. He stopped at the edge of the deck and smiled at her. Sara paused, wanting to throw herself at him, but didn't know if he was hurt.

"Hi."

"Hey, baby," he greeted back.

"Are you okay?"

He nodded. "I would be better if you came closer."

She laughed and wrapped her arms around his waist. Clint sighed at the first touch and his body relaxed. He embraced her and she tilted her head so when his lips came down, they shared a sweet kiss. Just one touch had her blood pumping and she moaned into his mouth. He gripped the back of her shirt, pressing her closer. They broke away from each other and she stared up at him.

"I'm so glad to see you tonight," she told him. Sara knew it was selfish to need him in her arms, but she didn't care.

"I couldn't go home until I checked on you," Clint told her.

She ran her hands over his chest. "So maybe you can stay? We were supposed to have dinner, but we could change that to breakfast if you want. Or if you're hungry, I made a pot of chili. How does that sound with a cold beer?"

He licked his lips. "I want."

"Which option?" she asked, with a smile.

"I want to stay. Have breakfast in the morning. Maybe the chili and beer later tonight."

"What do you need right now?"

"You."

She rose to her toes and kissed him again. This time, he was the one who moaned. Sara was going to take such good care of him that he'd never want to leave

"Come inside." She led him back to the door by his hand.

Ryan stood in the kitchen, waiting.

"Hey, man. I appreciate you staying with them," Clint said.

"Oh, I didn't mind one bit," Ryan confessed with a huge grin.

"Cecil?"

Ryan nodded.

"Good for you." Clint slapped Ryan on the back.

"I'm going to take him home. Give you two a little privacy," Ryan told them and headed back to the living room to collect Cecil.

"That's be great," Clint replied. Sara nodded her agreement.

Clint kept his arm around her shoulders while they saw their friends off. Cecil had even given Clint a small hug, welcoming him back. Sara grew a little emotional seeing her favorite people had bonded. But it was the bounce in Cecil's step as Ryan led him out of the door that made her smile.

Once the door closed, Clint turned her to face him. She was surprised with the emotion that showed plainly on his face and in his eyes.

"What's wrong?" she asked.

"There's something we need to talk about before I take you to bed."

"Okay." Sara wanted to get him naked to ensure he wasn't injured.

"I know we haven't known each other long, but I have to confess I want see where this goes. I want to be with you," he said.

She cupped his face. "I've already started to fall for you. I want to be with you, too."

"I'm accepting a permanent position here. I'll be staying."

"I'm glad." That took care of one of her concerns. He was making it so easy to care for him. Even know he was trying to make sure she knew the risk of being with him.

"There's still a danger," he said. "A chapter of the Church is opening close to here. You could be in danger."

"Clint—"

"You need to think about that," he interrupted. "I may always be a target. That means you will be, too, if we're together."

"I don't have to think about it," she said, curling her hands into his shirt. "My dad's the sheriff. That already puts me in the line of fire. And I'm not willing to give you up because of what *might* happen."

"I want you to be sure."

"Can you tell me about what happened today? About the danger? Not because I'd consider not being with you, but so I know."

"I'll tell you everything I can," he said. "There's more to the shifters here than you are aware."

"Ryan explained about the Council and your job," Sara told him.

"Well, that's convenient." Clint chuckled.

"I think he was trying to assure me that you could handle what was going on."

"I'm glad he was with you and that you talked to him. The people who work on the compound are my pack."

"Especially Kurt."

"Yes, he's more than my best friend," Clint confirmed. "We've been a team a long time."

"Will he stay?"

"Yes. We'll both take permanent positions here. I may have to travel from time to time. There's nothing I can do about that. But for the most part, I'll be here taking care of the Council and any shifters brought to the compound. This is where the trials against shifters take place."

"I understand you might have to go help other Packs. Ryan told me some of what you've done. I want to be the one that you come home to."

"That's what I was hoping for."

Sara pulled his shirt from the waistband of his jeans. "But right now, I need to make sure you're okay."

Clint lifted his arms. "I'll all yours. As long as you know the risks you're taking by being with me."

"I understand, I suggest that you will just have to keep a close eye on me. Maybe even..." She leaned close and rubbed against him suggestively.

"Oh, yeah," he murmured and brought his mouth down on hers.

This kiss was deeper than the earlier ones had been. Passionate and seductive. Clint moved his hands around and down until he cupped her ass and raised her up.

She wrapped her arms around his neck and lifted her legs to his waist. Her back hit the door and she rocked into his hold. Clint's mouth left hers and he nipped and sucked down her neck.

"Gonna mark you, make you mine," he whispered.

"Yours," she replied, grinding down. She was wet and ready.

He thrust up and she gasped.

"Take me to bed," she pleaded.

Without releasing her neck or letting her down, her carried her to the bedroom. Once there he fell onto the bed, twisting at the last minute so he hit the comforter with her on top.

She straddled his waist and threw her hair back. He pushed up her shirt and clamped his lips over her breast. She arched back, burying her hands in his hair.

They took their time undressing each other. Hands slid on sweaty skin, lips kissed, tongues tasted, slow and intense.

"Wait," she panted.

Clint stilled his previously busy hands.

She gazed down at him. There wasn't a mark on him. "They didn't hurt you?"

"No," Clint confirmed. "I was tied up for a while. The guy heading up this area wanted me to bite him and turn him into one of us."

"I thought that wasn't possible."

"It's not. I tried to tell him, but he demanded that I bite him."

"So, you bit him," she guessed. "I hope you made it hurt."

"Oh, I did."

Sara laughed. "Good." She ran her hands up his chest. His skin was so soft and tight. Looking down at his abs, she licked her lips. Soon, she wanted to spend the entire night worshipping every inch of him.

"Touch me," he ordered.

She was already doing so. Sara sat back on his legs so his shaft was in front of her. With a firm grip, she wrapped her fist around him. He bucked up. Running her thumb over the head of his erection, she spread the pre-cum there.

"You gonna ride me?" he asked.

"Yes," she said.

When she couldn't stand another second of not having him, she rose and grasped his cock. She shifted into position and lowered herself. Clint gripped her hips hard and she loved that strength. Once he was inside, she rocked a few times before she lifted up a little. She started to ride him at an unhurried pace.

Clint snapped his hips up and matched her rhythm. He panted under her, giving drawn-out moans of craving. She sped up a little, slamming down and placing her hands over his well-defined chest for balance.

God, there had never been another time that making love had felt so good, so right.

Her hair fell into her face. It became a curtain around them as Clint grabbed her face to bring her down for an excited kiss.

Harder, faster. That was all she could think about. More, she needed more.

She didn't realize she had spoken out loud until Clint flipped her back onto the mattress and plunged deep inside at a more rapid pace. He thrust and drove into her while she cried out for him. Sweat dripped from his face to her neck. He pushed her knees farther up to her chest.

Yes! Yes! She was almost there. Sara sobbed out once she was pushed over the edge into completion.

"So good." She rubbed her hands over his pecs, digging her nails in a little He hissed but thrust again and again.

"Come inside me," she ordered.

Clint snapped his hips a few more times before he roared out his own release. He collapsed on top of her, panting.

Holy hell, that had been amazing. Yeah, there was no doubt she would be keeping him around for a very long time. She whimpered while he began to pull out, wanting to keep the connection with him.

"We're at the wrong end of the bed," he commented with amusement.

"Humph," she grunted. Like she cared.

He laughed and lifted and moved her so her head was on a pillow and the sheet covered her. He settled next to her and wrapped one strong arm around her waist to pull her close.

She reached down and entwined their fingers together. Her eyes were still closed and she was sleepy—a wonderful, deep, contented exhaustion from spent passion.

Oh, yeah. She planned on ending every night like this.

Just then, his stomach growled loud enough to echo in the silent room.

"One hunger sated, now time for the next?" she teased. Sara opened her eyes. She'd wanted to cuddle, but she needed to take care of him even more.

"I do need to eat," he said. "I can't actually remember the last thing I had."

Sara sat up.

"Lie back down," he said. He tried to push her back. "If you don't mind, I'll make me a snack to tide me over."

"I do mind!" she said. "Come on."

He groaned, but allowed her to pull him off the mattress. Sara walked over to her dresser and yanked out a pair of pajama bottoms and a tank. She dressed without underwear, but she didn't plan on being in clothes long. She watched over her shoulder as Clint pulled on his boxer briefs.

"I'll warm you up a bowl of chili and you can tell me the rest of what happened today."

He nodded. "I should have told you earlier. Bobby Gibson has disappeared."

"They took him?" she asked. Damn, Bobby was the newest deputy, but she'd known him a long time.

"No," Clint said. He strolled over and pulled him into an embrace. "He was the one waiting for me behind your shop. He's working with the other humans."

She gasped. "After everything my dad did for him, he betrayed us?"

Clint grinned. "Us?"

"If he betrayed you, then he betrayed all of us," she stated. Sara pulled him down the hall. "Now, let me feed you."

"Do I still get a beer?"

"Sure."

Chapter Nine

Clint peered round the room at the guards he'd now be working with full time. Ryan grinned at him from the opposite side of the table. Alpha Babcock had just announced the new positions. As expected, the other guards appeared to be pleased with Kurt and Clint assuming new roles. Clint had even more in store for them. He was going to make certain the men and women under his command were the strongest and bravest.

Kurt rose and shook hands with Alpha Babcock, then turned to the rest of the shifters. There was a mix of male and female guards, the only ones missing currently watching the property. Kurt and he would meet with them later.

"Priority one is going to be cleaning up the town," Kurt stated. "With Perry Costa and his men in custody, the sheriff's department has their hands full. Plus, don't forget that we're still looking for one of the deputies."

"Here's a picture of Bobby Gibson," Clint said. He stood and passed the photo around. "Those of you who hang around town will probably recognize him. He was directly involved with Perry's men." He wouldn't allow Bobby to remain free after betraying those who had cared and trusted him. Plus Bobby was a threat to Sara. Clint couldn't allow anything or anyone to remain a danger to her.

"We're setting up a rotation to search the woods and in town. When you're not looking for Gibson, you'll be here at the compound on guard duty or in training. We all know that Dan Carter is setting up a church less than twenty miles away. That's too close for my comfort," Kurt stated. "We're currently looking at identifying all the members of the church so we can be on the lookout for them. We made a promise to this town to always protect them and we will."

One of the guards raised his hand.

"Yes, Bennet?" Kurt asked.

"Are we all in danger of being kidnapped?" Bennet asked.

Clint and Kurt exchanged a look. This was what they'd hoped to avoid. It would be hard for the newer guards to concentrate on their jobs if they were worried about Carter's plans. Bennet had only been at the compound for four months. Clint would have been happier with more experienced guards than what they had. At the moment, half the compounds guards were seasoned, but the remaining needed a lot of training. Which was Clint's job.

"I can't answer that," Kurt said. "It's possible that we are all targets. We still have a job to do, though. Plus, working in teams will ensure everyone remains safe.

You have to remember the original plan was to make Clint and I vulnerable. It won't be the same this time."

"Okay." Bennet nodded but looked nervous.

Clint walked around the table to join Kurt. "Part of your duties here will be to train more. I'll oversee this aspect. If you'd like more one-on-one classes, I'll be happy to oblige. I will also be bringing in some friends of mine who specialize."

"That's great." Ryan spoke up. "I, for one, would love to expand my skills."

Several others were agreeing, both vocally and with nods.

Clint was pleased. He'd spoken earlier that morning with his friends Mike and RJ who'd come to assist him. They were both highly trained military men and had been more than happy to help. "I'll post the schedule tomorrow."

Alpha Babcock stood. "There's going to be a lot of changes coming up in the next few months. Dan Carter and people like him are a real threat. But don't forget that not all humans are like them. The majority of the people you come across will accept you. Don't lose focus and don't let fear dictate your relationships."

"I agree," Kurt said. "These are our humans. Let's keep them safe."

The short meeting adjourned, Clint was hopeful the men and women who'd be working under him would approach the next few months with an open mind. Sara was one of the humans who needed protecting. She'd always been kind and welcoming to the shifters from the compound. She and the other residents deserved respect.

"I can't tell you two how happy I am that you've accepted our offer," Alpha Babcock stated. He shook first Kurt's hand then Clint's.

"It's a pleasure," Kurt replied. "This is a good place to make a home."

Plus the money wasn't bad, either. Clint had always been paid well doing jobs for the Council. When he'd arrived that morning, Kurt had handed him a written offer from the Council. Double the salary he'd been making, plus money for living expenses. Later that day, he and Kurt were going to look at houses in the area. They also had the choice to stay at the compound if they wanted. It had been Kurt's idea to at least see what their options were.

Alpha Babcock exited the room and Clint turned to his friend.

"Are you ready to look at houses?" Kurt asked.

"Yep." Clint headed for the door.

"You're sure?" Kurt questioned. "At the rate you're going with Sara, it won't be too long before you live together.

Clint grinned. "As soon as I can manage it."

"Then why are we looking at houses?" Kurt asked. "I didn't think about it this morning, but really it doesn't make sense. I can stay here."

He was quick to shake his head. "This isn't about a house, and you know it," Clint said. "This is where we'll spend our free time. Eventually raising a family. You can't do that from the compound."

"Then I should get my own place," Kurt said. "You can stay with me until Sara finally takes your sorry ass in."

Clint ignored Kurt's joking. "No, we'll be able to afford a nicer place together. Plus, I have to approve of it. I can't let my pups hang around some rundown shack."

"Pups now?" Kurt teased. "We're talking about pups?"

"We're talking about whatever Sara lets me have."

Kurt pulled his keys from his pocket as he caught up to Clint. "At least you admit it. I always knew it would be a special woman who caught you. Sara's perfect for you."

"I agree," Clint stated. "Now, let's go find a place that I can woo her at."

"Oh, God!" Kurt complained. "Don't ever say those words again."

"What? I heard wooing is back in style."

He ducked his head when Kurt took a swipe at him. They were laughing as they exited the large compound. Clint peered around from the large steps leading to the entrance. The land surrounding him flourished with life and sacrifices of the shifters who had come before him.

All members of a Pack had a special connection to the territory that accepted them. Alphas even more so. But this property, the land that surrounded it, was magical. Having an entire Council of Alphas supporting the territory had power coursing through each blade of grass, among every other touch of nature. Clint had never felt that influence before.

Something had changed when Alpha Babcock had taken him and Kurt into the Pack.

Clint shuddered as he stood, connecting the gift of the territory.

His blood pumped. Inside, he could feel his wolf gaining strength, and each heightened sense seemed to expand. "Wow," he murmured.

"I had no idea..." Kurt said.

So, his best friend was feeling the same sense of awe as him. Clint couldn't take his gaze from the scenery to glance at Kurt, though. Instead, he kept his eyes locked on the sway of the limbs on the large old trees that surrounded him.

The energy pulsing inside him almost forced a shift. He didn't know if he could stop the transformation from happening.

"I think we're going to have to put off our house hunting for right now," Kurt said. "We have to run."

"Thank God!" Clint was already pulling his shirt over his head.

Once he'd dropped all articles of clothing to the ground, the transformation took root.

He was used to shifting often, but this change was different. While there was never pain for him as he transformed, he knew it was faster. Clint circled, not quite certain how different this shift was. Was he bigger? He felt like he was at least taller.

Clint turned to find Kurt and couldn't believe his eyes. *Fuck!* Oh, yeah, their transformation had been affected. Kurt was huge! His best friend was peering back at him, looking as shocked.

With a nudge, Clint urged Kurt to move. He needed to run. The land around him was calling to some part of Clint that he'd never felt before. Kurt raised his head and howled. Instinct had Clint adding his voice.

Once their howls trailed off, Kurt ran. Clint stumbled to follow, his feet sliding on the stone steps, until he jumped onto the grass. His nails dug into the dirt before he launched himself after his friend.

The breeze ruffled the fur on his back. It was almost like the wind was pushing him forward, toward something. He could see Kurt's large body ahead of him so he hurried to catch up. Under the canopy of the full leaves, the light darkened, even though it was only midmorning. The air was fresher, as well. Instead of the stench of iron, metal and concrete, there was nothing but life and energy that he could pick up.

This was amazing.

Clint had made this same run many times in the last few months, but never had he experienced the feeling of belonging as he did now.

It was almost like the land had been waiting for them.

For the first time in many years, Clint allowed the human side of his mind to drift, which let the animal instinct take over. He was still aware of everything around him, but he'd given the wolf full rein.

Instead of seeing the broken limbs of trees or fallen foliage, Clint noticed the ruts in the dirt made by smaller animals. Made by prey. His mouth watered as he imagined finding a rabbit or something similar. He was a hunter, after all.

Movement out of the corner of his eye caught his attention and he paused. Clint dropped to his belly and rested his chin on his paws. He didn't even twitch a muscle. With the patience of a hunter, he waited.

There was only the sound of smaller critters scurrying about, the birds above his head and the gentle sway of the branches. It was so peaceful that now the adrenaline was leaving him that he could have napped. But that wasn't what he wanted. Concentrating on his prey, he caught the scent of the rabbit.

It was coming right for him.

He positioned his legs under his heavy body in preparation.

Clint held in a growl. He so wanted to play, to chase, to catch.

As the little animal hopped forward, it wasn't aware of the predator in wait. Clint lifted his ass end even gave a little wiggle. Just as he prepared to pounce, Kurt leapt in front of him, scaring off Clint's prize.

Clint grunted in disappointment, the human part taking over again, allowing his wolf instincts to fade. Which was a good thing, since his wolf part might have been stupid enough to attack Kurt. The loss of prey was maddening.

Clint shook his massive head and blinked. Oh, shit, he'd almost caught a rabbit. Ugh, it wasn't like he'd never had to survive on his wolf hunting before, but Clint didn't enjoy it. He preferred to eat the human way.

Rumbling, Kurt lowered his head to Clint's from where he crouched. Yeah, if Clint had to guess, he'd say Kurt had been aware Clint had given his wolf free range. His best friend was also aware that the human part of Clint did not want to munch down on any critters.

He bumped his forehead against Kurt's before grinning. Or as much as he could, transformed into a wolf. Kurt nudged him back, then looked over his shoulder. It was time to run again. Then they would have to shift back and get on with their day. Clint rose back to his feet, then stretched out his back. Kurt glanced at him before taking off once again. This time, Clint followed behind, not letting himself get caught up in his wolf.

* * * *

It was after lunch when Clint and Kurt showed up at her shop. Sara finished making three caramel salted mochas before looking up at the two shifters.

"Angie!" she called. "Your order is ready."

The pixie-looking blonde teenager bounced up to the counter, then took the drinks. Sara waited until Angie and her two friends had exited the shop before going around the counter and straight into Clint's arms. She'd already let Cecil go for the day since she'd be closing up soon.

"Hey," Clint greeted her with warmth. His embrace was tight but comfortable.

"You smell like fresh grass," she commented.

He chuckled. "I bet I do. I probably should have showered before coming."

"Oh, no," she told him. "I like it." Sara pulled back and peer up at him. "Did you shift?"

"You could say that," Kurt replied.

Clint smiled. "We were accepted into the Alpha Pack today. It was amazing. I've never felt so much power before."

Now that she was looking at him, Clint appeared a little different to her. She raised her hand to brush the skin under his eyes. "The lines are gone."

"I know," Clint said. "We realized it earlier after our run, but none of the Alphas were around to ask. Kurt's going to check back with them after we're done for the day."

"Oh? And what's the plan for today?" she asked.

"House hunting." With a happy smile, Clint nodded. "You know, so we have a place to live."

It was on the tip of Sara's tongue to tell him that he already had a place. There was plenty of room for Kurt at her house, as well. But it was too soon. Shit, it hadn't even been a week since they'd first gotten together. Why did it seem like so much longer?

The flirting and getting to know each other had taken months since Clint had gotten to Lovington, but their relationship still hadn't been going long. She couldn't invite Clint to move in already. Even if it was what she wanted.

"What kind of place are you looking for?" she asked.

"A house." Kurt spoke up. "Something that isn't too far from the compound, but not in the middle of town, either."

"Or you," Clint added.

She grinned. "I know the place. That is, if you don't mind putting in some work."

Clint and Kurt exchanged glances. They both shook their heads.

"That would be great," Kurt said. "Give me something to do in my free time."

Clint snorted. "Because we're going to have so much of that?"

"I need a project," Kurt commented.

"At least take a look at it before you decide," Sara said. "If you don't like the old Meadows' place, there are plenty of more houses I can show you. Although they're closer to town."

Kurt shrugged. "Sounds good to me."

"Just let me close up," she told them. "Do you want a drink while you wait?"

"No," Clint said. "We'll help."

"If you could put the chairs on top of the tables, I'll sweep," she directed. Sara made her way back behind the counter and began to clean up the blender area after that last order. Cecil had already done almost everything else, so it shouldn't take longer than fifteen minutes to finish up.

"Where's the broom?" Clint asked as he stepped up to the bar.

"Behind the door." Sara pointed. Kurt already had half the chairs picked up.

Working as a team, it took only ten minutes before she was carrying the cash drawer to her office. She could do the deposit the next day. Right now, she was excited to show Kurt and Clint the old Meadow house. Ralph and Kristen Meadow had left town when the shifters had announced their presence. Unbeknownst to them, their daughter had mated with a cougar shifter. Once Susan Meadow had informed her parents of her new family, they'd moved to be closer, leaving a beautiful home less than a mile from Sara.

She entered the office, leaving Kurt and Clint to wait up front. Or at least she'd thought until Clint stepped up behind her. He placed his hands on her hips, then drew her back. His erection brushed against her ass.

"You wanting something other than to look at houses?" she asked. It was near impossible not to wiggle in a tease, so she didn't.

Clint tightened his fingers. "Kurt stepped out to give us a few minutes. He's going to make sure none of Carter's men are still around."

"Ohhhhh." Sara placed the drawer on her desk before turning to face Clint. "Just a few minutes."

Clint lifted her until she sat on her desk. "That's all we need. I want you too much."

She loved the way Clint needed her. And he was so honest about it. No playing games. Clint told her what he wanted. Sara pressed her hands against the thin cotton of his T-shirt. Beneath her palms, she could feel his heart racing.

He slid his hands up her thighs until she was spread. Too bad she still wore her jeans. "Clint."

"Lie back," he ordered.

"Sure." With a wicked grin, she did as he'd said.

Clint pushed up her shirt until her breasts were revealed. With a flick of his fingers, her bra loosened. He arched up, offering her skin to his mouth. He licked his lips. "I love your body."

That was a damn good thing in her opinion.

"Let me worship you," he said.

"Whatever you want," she told him. "Anything."

"Lift up," he said.

She complied. Clint pulled down her jeans and panties but hadn't removed her shoes. The clothes got caught up at her ankles. Sara struggled to toe off her shoes. He laughed at her, then helped her. Once her jeans dropped to the floor, he stepped between her legs.

He was hard for her. Sara reached for his zipper, but Clint caught her hand. "Not yet."

"Come on," she urged. Sara lifted her hips. "Now."

Instead of releasing her wrist, he used his free hand to trail through the slick folds covering her pussy. Sara moaned. He slipped one finger inside. "Yes!" she hissed.

Clint plunged first one digit then another inside her. As good as it felt, she wanted his cock. For him to lay claim to her body.

"I'm ready," she practically yelled.

He chuckled before finally, finally, undoing the button of his pants. When he released his cock, Sara once again reached for him. This time, Clint allowed her to wrap her hand around his length and stroke. He filled her palm, but the heat that seared into her flesh called to her.

"I want you to take me," Sara said. "Right now."

"Yes, now." He replaced her hand with his, then moved forward until he was pressed against her.

Sara lifted her arms above her head and gripped the edge of the wooden desk. He entered her slowly until he was buried all the way inside. Clint paused as he peered down at her.

"Keep your eyes on me," he told her.

She nodded.

He withdrew before thrusting back in. The rock of his hips started gently but quickly grew in force and speed. She strained to meet each plunge until sweat pooled on her forehead. It was hot in the office and Clint was making her burn with passion. It wasn't until he bent over her, hands tight, and lost the control he'd been holding in that she let herself get lost in the feel of him.

Every time they met, the slap of skin echoed and their moans rose.

Sara's orgasm had her lifting up and wrapping her arms around Clint's shoulder. He still rode her, not slowing down, until he began to come. Sara grinned when Clint dropped down. He wasn't quite crushing her, but she wouldn't be able to lie there for long.

"That was good," he panted.

"Good," she agreed. "You can say that again."

Clint chuckled. "And again and again."

Sara shook her head. "Not here, though. You're crushing my ribs."

With a groan he pushed up, hovering over her. "Better?"

"Move!" She shoved at his chest until he backed away. "I don't want Kurt to walk in and find both of us naked."

"Like he'd even try," Clint said. "He knows what we're doing."

"Oh, really?" She lifted a brow. "So you told your friend that you were following me back to my office so we can have hot monkey sex on my desk?"

"Monkey sex?" Clint asked. "I don't have sex like a monkey." He sounded put out.

Giggling, she managed to roll off the desk. Her jeans had gotten kicked across the room. She stomped over to them, already feeling the exhaustion of the day. She'd worked a full shift, then Clint had totally rocked her world. All she wanted to do was crawl into bed and take a nap. Maybe she could talk Clint into joining her after they looked at the Meadows' house.

* * * *

Clint had let Kurt drive and Sara sit in the passenger side, so he was the last to look at the house. But the way that Kurt gasped and Sara giggled had him peering through the seats ahead of them.

The light-blue structure looked down at them from a small hill. It would be the perfect location to see if anyone was coming from all directions. Easily defendable.

"This is it?" Kurt asked.

Clint could already hear the interest in Kurt's tone. It was a good-looking house. As they got closer, Clint could see that repairs were, in fact, needed. The porch railing sat at an angle. Several of the steps had holes in them.

"The inside is in good shape. A year before the Meadows moved, Ralph suffered a heart attack. Most of us stopped by and helped as we could. Cooking, mowing the yard, things like that," Sara said.

"That's nice of everyone," Clint told her.

"Community," Sara said. "Ralph got better. By the time he'd started working on the house, the shifters announced their presence. Then their daughter came home and told them about mating with a shifter. They immediately packed up to join her and her new family."

"So they support shifters," Kurt said. "That means they shouldn't have a problem with selling their house to us."

"Come on," Sara said. "I know where the key is." She pushed open her door.

"What do you think?" Clint asked.

"I love it."

"You haven't even seen the inside yet," Clint pointed out.

Kurt laughed. "I can't explain it. I feel like this is where I'm supposed to be."

"Then let's take a look." Clint clasped Kurt's shoulder, then climbed out of the back seat. Sara stood in front of the vehicle, waiting on them. He joined her before pulling her against his side.

Looking up at the house, Clint could admit that it was nice, but he wasn't feeling whatever Kurt was. He wanted a home, but Clint already knew where he wanted to end up. This was only a stop for him.

"Kurt already loves it," Sara said. She watched his best friend prowl around the yard. "What do you think?"

He shrugged. "It's nice."

Sara turned in his arms. "But you're going to live here?"

"It's better than staying at the compound. And this is closer to you."

"Yes, it is," she agreed.

"So, I'll still get to spend my free time with you."

"That you're not going to have a lot of." She repeated his earlier words.

"With Carter's churches growing and the threat to the town, there's a lot going on. I'm also starting a more intense training schedule for the guards."

"But you'll be here," Sara said. "In Lovington."

"I don't plan to go anywhere. If I do get sent to help another Pack, then I have someone to return to."

"Oh, you better return to me." She wrapped her arms around his neck. "I'll hunt you down if you don't."

"Hunt me down?" he asked. It was funny that she'd used those words. He was the known hunter, after all.

"Let's see the rest." Kurt joined them.

"Follow me." Sara started toward the house.

"Watch the steps!" Clint hollered. He rushed up to take her arm.

"It's fine," she told him.

"No." He pulled her back. "Let me go first."

She was frowning at him but allowed Clint to hold her arm as they made their way to the front door. Sara stopped to bend down and move a planter where a key was hidden.

"Really?" Clint asked dubiously.

She laughed. "Everyone knows it's there."

He huffed out a breath but took the key from her before handing it over to Kurt. "Well, go ahead."

Kurt stared at the metal in his hand for several moments, then snatched it. Clint was a little taken back at how much this property was affecting his best friend. Kurt didn't normally get attached like this.

He stood back, holding on to Sara, in case the interior wasn't as sturdy as she believed. Kurt glanced back over his shoulder. Clint nodded.

"It is safe," Sara said. "The inside's fine."

Kurt pushed open the door, then stepped over the threshold. Clint waited.

Sara huffed and followed. Clint didn't release her arm but let her take a few steps. He peered around the entrance to see Kurt stopped in the middle of the entry.

"Come on." Kurt motioned to him. "She's right."

Sara just laughed. He and Clint went into the house as Kurt strolled forward. The furniture had already been removed, so there were only wide-open spaces. But the floors were hardwood and still in good condition. Even the paint on the walls wasn't bad, although eggshell was not something he'd want to live with.

"What do you think about knocking down some walls and opening this place up?" Kurt asked.

Clint looked around. Yeah, he could picture what Kurt was talking about.

"The kitchen is pretty awesome," Sara said. He dragged him behind her and Kurt followed.

She was right. Cabinets that matched the floors, an elegant marble island in the middle and new appliances.

"How many bedrooms?" Kurt asked.

"Three or four," she said.

"Let's go upstairs," Clint suggested.

"I get the master," Kurt stated. "Since I'll be here more, you know."

Clint laughed. "I sure the hell hope so."

Sara rolled her eyes. "Smooth."

The three of them tromped across the house until they got to the stairs. Gray carpet covered each step. It was the first place of the house that had carpet. Clint led the way until he reached the top. There were five doors up there. He walked over to the first and pushed it open. A good-sized room. Next door was a closet, then a bathroom. Across the hall a smaller bedroom, then at the end was the master suite.

Kurt whistled as he made a circle around the master suite. "I like it."

Clint stepped over to the window. There was a nice view of the woods that separated the house from the compound. "I can't think of any reason not to make an offer," he said. Clint turned to Sara. "They'll rent it?"

"Sell," Kurt said fast.

He turned to his best friend.

"I want this place," Kurt said. "I want to own the land."

"Sure." Clint rubbed his hands over his face. It wasn't going to be easy to get the structure ready, find Bobby and train. Clint didn't think he would have much time with Sara. And that did not make him happy.

"I'll give you their number," Sara said. "The Meadows are good people. I bet if they accept your offer, they'll let you go ahead and start on the updates."

"We'll need some help," Clint said.

"The guards," Kurt said. "Some of them will be more than willing to help."

"Plus some of the town," Sara said. "A guy I went to high school with has a painting business. He's done the community center and school. Several residents have used him. He's pretty good."

"Great," Kurt said. "If you get me the number, I'll talk to him after I call the Meadows."

"Okay." Sara waved her hand. "Are you sure that you don't want to look at any other houses?"

Clint agreed. This was the only place that they'd had seen.

"I'm certain. I want to call the owners tonight," Kurt said.

Sara bounced on the tip of her toes. "I'm kind of excited." She laughed.

Kurt nodded. "Me, too."

"We can go back to my house and I'll give you the number. I'll also make us some lunch."

Clint's stomach growled.

"I'll take that as a yes," she joked.

"Feed me, woman!" Clint used his best caveman voice.

The smile that broke out on her face was amazing. Kurt clamped him on the shoulder. It felt good to be standing in the room with the two people who meant the most to him. It was still astounding that everything he'd ever wanted was within his reach. The fact that Kurt and Sara got along so well meant something to him. He needed them to be close.

There was still a threat to the town, though.

Kurt led the way to the front door. Clint held Sara's hand as they exited. He wanted to keep her close until Bobby Gibson was found. In the meantime, he had guards making trips around Sara's house just to be sure Sara wasn't targeted.

Bobby had every reason to go after Sara now. His cover was blown in town. All he had was Carter's men and the church. Most of the shifters thought Bobby was with Carter's crew. Clint didn't think so, though. He had this feeling that as soon as he let his guard down, Bobby would pop up.

Chapter Ten

Clint wiped the sweat from his brow as he reached the street. The morning was cold, but with his shifter blood it isn't too much for him to handle. Dressed in a pair of running pants and a sweatshirt, along with a beanie, he was quite comfortable.

He stopped at the post office to check his PO box and collect his mail.

"Clint!"

Glancing over his shoulder, he spotted Mrs. Garcia waving at him from the door. Clint grabbed the few pieces of mail then locked up. He rushed over to where the older lady was waiting on him.

"Mrs. Garcia," he said. "Is everything okay?"

"Of course." She patted his shoulder. "I wanted to make sure you boys were doing all right."

"We are," Clint said.

"I heard you boys are buying the old Meadow place," she said.

"That was quick," he muttered. Kurt had left him a voice message that he'd spoken to Ralph Meadow and the man was more than willing to sell. He'd stopped by the compound after leaving Sara's that morning, but Kurt had been in a meeting with the Alphas so Clint went for his morning run. Okay, he wanted to see Sara. But he still needed exercise.

"Small town," Mrs. Garcia said. "I wanted to let you know that my grandson has a painting business. He does very good work. I would make him give you a good deal."

"It wouldn't happen to be George's, would it?" Clint asked. He was already smiling.

"Yes! You've heard of him?"

"I believe Kurt is calling him this morning," Clint said. "Sara told us about him. That was who she recommended."

"That girl." Mrs. Garcia grinned. "Such a good girl."

"She is," Clint agreed.

"I'll let you go. I'll talk to my George and tell him to treat you good."

Clint had no doubt that even without Mrs. Garcia's word George would take care of them. Still, he needed to get used to the small town. It was like a Pack. People coming together and helping. Everyone knowing everyone else's business. He had to open himself up to the humans like he did his Pack.

"Okay, Mrs. Garcia," Clint said. "You have a good day, ma'am."

"You, too." She hurried down the sidewalk. Wow, she moved pretty damn well for a woman who had to be in her late seventies. Amazing.

He turned, then headed toward Sara's shop. There was a steady stream of people going in and out. With the weather taking an even bigger turn toward the cold, it wasn't surprising that the residents of Lovington needed something to warm them up.

He held the open door as two young teens came rushing out. They were laughing and joking but stopped to apologize real quick before going on their way. Clint shook his head, then made his way toward the counter.

Cecil worked the espresso machine as Sara visited with the customers.

"Hey, handsome," Sara greeted. She leaned over the counter and kissed him right there in front of everyone.

Well, if the town wasn't aware of their relationship before, they would be now. Clint was proud. Sara had just claimed him.

"You're sweaty," she complained. But she smiled.

"That's what happens when you go running," he said. "Having a good morning?"

"I am," she said. "Now suck on this."

It was probably a good thing that the customers had all gone to sit, because Clint moaned at her words. "What is it?" he asked as he pulled the frozen drink toward him. "And why are you making frozen drinks on a day like this?"

"It's frozen hot chocolate," she said. "Cecil found the recipe online and we thought we would try it out. It's pretty good."

A frozen hot chocolate. Well, Clint would give it a try if she wanted him to. "If I drink this, can I have my regular?"

She laughed. "I promise. Just tell me what you think."

He took a sip. Then another. Not bad, not bad at all.

"He likes it!" Cecil pointed. "I knew it."

Surprisingly the drink was really good. With a rich flavor and creamy smooth texture. While he'd never been a fan of hot chocolate, since he preferred to get his caffeine from coffee, he could see himself indulging in this treat every once in a while.

"I think you should add it to the menu," he told them.

"Already done," Sara said. She glanced over at Cecil. "When Cecil has a good idea, I've learned to listen. Most of the unique combinations on the menu are his."

Clint nodded. He was reaching for his large cup of coffee when his cell rang. He frowned and pulled his phone from his pocket.

"Hey, Kurt," he said. "Want me to bring you a coffee?"

"I got a call from one of the guards. He thinks he might have spotted Bobby Gibson outside the woods."

Clint stepped away from counter to a quiet corner of the shop. "Where?" He had a bad feeling.

"Three blocks from Sara's house," Kurt replied. "It was one of the guards going between the compound and Sara's who called."

"Fuck," he spat. "I'm on my way."

"I think we should approach him from the compound side. I'm going to shift and bring some of the other guards with me. You come in from the south."

"You want me to shift, as well?" he asked.

"No, you can come in as human. If you enter behind Sara's block, you shouldn't be seen. The guard thinks Gibson is there to stay for a while, so that should give us plenty of time to get into position."

"I'm leaving now," he said. Clint disconnected the call.

Sara was around the counter and holding his cup out to him. "Everything okay?"

"Yeah, should be. I have to go, but I'll see you later?"

"You'll come by tonight?" she asked.

Clint hadn't spent a night away from her. He didn't plan to unless she told him that was what she wanted. "How about I bring dinner tonight?" he asked. It was normal for Sara to provide their evening meal, but he wanted to do something for her. Since he couldn't cook, the next best thing would be to bring her something.

She perked up. "Pizza?"

Damn, she was perfect. "Pepperoni?"

"Yes, please."

He leaned in and gave her a quick kiss. Hopefully he could get Bobby in custody of the sheriff and pick up dinner on time. "I'll see you later."

Clint strolled down the sidewalk, heading in the direction he'd need to go without trying to draw attention to himself. Just heading out after seeing his girl and grabbing a cup of coffee. That was what he wanted the residents to think.

He was both disturbed and relieved to get the call on Bobby. Relieved that they could out the man behind bars where he belonged. But it pissed him off that he'd been right about Bobby being a danger to Sara. Why else would he be in her neighborhood?

Clint knew that it would be a real test in his control when he was in front of Bobby. This was the deputy who'd betrayed all of them. Bobby had turned his back on the town that had taken him in and accepted him as one of their own. He might have gotten Clint, but Bobby Gibson was a coward.

Taking a drink of his coffee, he had to smile. Sara did brew the best cup he'd ever tasted. He could barely stomach the crap that he managed to make.

Quick, he downed the cooling brew before he tossed the cup into a trashcan.

Now that he was getting off the main street, he could pick up his pace. He jogged across the road to follow the trail that would lead him to where Bobby should be hiding out. He was going to have to use his senses to sniff out the man, but that would be fun. A little hunting before they took Gibson down once and for all.

Once surrounded by the forest, Clint stopped and breathed deep. It was true that his senses weren't as strong in his human form, but he could still find his prey. This time, Kurt wouldn't be stepping in between him and his target. Clint wasn't going to allow Bobby Gibson to get away again.

He stepped over branches and around large boulders as he made his way north. Clint could still see the outline of the houses in the neighborhood. He was only a few blocks from Sara's. If he continued on the trail, he could even take it to the house that Kurt had fallen in love with. Clint was already thinking about it as being Kurt's.

This small town was going to be his home, one way or another. Already residents like Mrs. Garcia were making him feel welcome. To return the favor, Clint needed to ensure their safety.

A crack of a branch snapped to his left and Clint ducked behind a fallen log. His hand slipped on the moss that had collected and he bit back a curse. Still, he hunkered down to wait.

Shifter. Young. Male.

The scent that reached him was a little familiar. He grinned. One of the guards was heading in his direction. If Clint had been human, he'd never have heard the guard approaching. But this was going to be a good lesson for this young man to learn.

Clint shuffled around until he could get into position. He currently stood downwind, so luck was on his side. As the guard moved into his eyeline, Clint came up from behind. It was a simple task and Jody, indeed one of the youngest guards, who was normally on gate patrol, instincts should be screaming at him. Instead Jody walked forward, appearing not to have a care in the world.

Yeah, Clint had a lot more training in store for his men and women.

He crept behind Jody. At the same time as he clamped a hand down on Jody's shoulder, he also covered the other shifter's mouth. A muffled yell was all that escaped.

"You will write me an essay for every wrong step you took," Clint whispered in Jody's ear. "Then we're going to go step by step and I'll teach you to be the best damn tracker in the Pack."

As soon as Clint started talking, Jody relaxed.

Clint chuckled. He released Jody and the young guard turned.

Jody was shaking his head. "Kurt sent me to find you. You weren't supposed to find me."

"I have more experience than you," Clint told him. "Where is our fearless leader?"

"Back that way." Jody pointed over his shoulder. "They haven't spotted Gibson yet. Do you think he took off?"

"No," Clint murmured. "He's hiding in here. Which is pretty stupid since us shifters thrive in nature." If Bobby had been smart, he'd have stayed away from where the shifters were patrolling.

Clint closed his eyes and concentrated on the forest surrounding him. His instincts told him to continue on his path. He waved for Jody to follow. Opening his eyes, he strolled quietly back in search of his prey.

It only took another ten minutes before Clint knew he'd chosen the right direction. He motioned for Jody to stop and crouch down. Luckily the young shifter followed his directions.

He could smell Gibson. The strong odor of unwashed flesh and fear.

Why hadn't he left with Carter's other people? What would be the purpose of staying in town? Clint didn't know. But he did know Gibson was terrified.

Good, the man should get a little taste of his own medicine before he was locked up for kidnapping. Using hand gestures that Jody would be able to follow, Clint directed the guard to circle around where Bobby was huddled against an old oak trunk. He was sleeping. Jesus, the fucking guy was asleep as Clint hunted for him.

Even as he shook his head, he stomped directly toward Bobby. He didn't even slow down. Merely strolled forward until he reached the human who wasn't aware of his presence.

"Wakey, wakey." He dropped to his knees so he was looming over Bobby.

Bobby fluttered his eyes, then opened them to look up at Clint. He started to scream, but Clint wrapped his hand around Bobby's throat.

"Nope," Clint growled. "No screaming."

The utter terror and desperation that wafted from Bobby had Clint needing to fight back every instinct telling him to tear the human limb from limb. But Clint wasn't a monster. Not like Dan Carter or the others thought he was.

He rose, pulling Bobby up along with him. Jody stepped around the tree, shaking his head.

"That was too easy," Jody said. It was obvious that he was disappointed. So was Clint.

"I know," Clint replied. "Maybe I should let him go. He could run and we can give chase."

"Even with a head start, he wouldn't be a real challenge," Jody argued.

Bobby was shaking and crying. His eye bugged out, even though Clint wasn't choking him. He held the man tighter, but Bobby could still breathe.

"But we already caught him once," Clint said. "That should count."

"Maybe if we had more targets?" Jody asked. "Does he have any family?"

Bobby pissed his pants.

"Fuck," Clint spat. He held Bobby farther away from his body.

"That's enough," Kurt stated as he joined them. "I swear you can corrupt anyone," Kurt said to Clint.

"What did I do?" Clint asked.

But Kurt was already reaching for Bobby. "The sheriff is waiting."

Clint allowed Kurt to take Bobby from his grasp. Bobby began to gasp for breath, but Clint didn't care. A little discomfort was the least that Bobby deserved.

"We have him now," Kurt said. Clint frowned at his best friend. "It's over."

"Fine." Clint threw up his arms. "I got better things to do anyway."

Jody bounced on the tip of his toes. "We can still have fun."

In response, Clint raised a brow. "I don't think that Kurt's going to let us play with the human."

"I'm not!" Kurt hollered from where he was dragging Bobby in the direction of the street.

"I was thinking of more of a game," Jody said. He looked at the other shifters that had come with Kurt. "For all of us."

"I'm intrigued," Clint said.

"Well, we're all heading back to the same place," Jody said. "Why don't we make it fun?"

"Race?" Ryan called out.

Jody rolled his eyes. "Because you're one of the fastest? No."

"Then what?" Ryan asked.

"Clint shifts and hides. Whoever finds him wins."

"Uh..." Ryan glanced around. "Maybe we should pick someone else."

"Are you saying that you won't be able to find me?" Clint taunted.

"Pretty sure none of us will," Ryan answered.

"Sure, you will," Clint promised. "I'll go easy on you. You only need to cover the distance between here and the compound." This sounded like fun. He had a few hours to kill before he was expected at Sara's and this could count as training. And it had been Jody's idea, which showed he had some real interest in bettering himself.

Ryan frowned.

"I'll make sure he doesn't cheat," Kurt said.

"I thought you were taking Bobby to the sheriff." Clint turned. "And I don't cheat."

"He really doesn't cheat," Kurt told the other guys. He looked over at Clint. "The sheriff and deputies were already on their way to us. We met with them and handed Bobby over. I'm sure Sheriff Webb can handle Bobby. He's still shaking with the fear you put in him."

"Good," Clint growled.

"Now, are you going to let me in on the fun?" Kurt asked. "I can make it more of a challenge for you and show these guys some tricks you're sure to use."

That would be better. "You stay human and the others shift," Clint said.

Kurt nodded. "Fine. But you only get a twenty-minute head start."

A real challenge. Clint clapped his hands together, then rubbed them. The excitement had begun the thrum through him. He tugged off his shirt before tossing it at Kurt.

Kurt laughed. "Don't get cocky. I'm getting better at hunting and I know your tricks."

"You *think* you know my tricks," Clint corrected. "I still have a few up my sleeve."

"Uh..." Ryan spoke up. "We'll be able to find you though, right?"

Clint gestured at the guards standing around watching him. "Trust your instincts. Follow your nose. If you use all your senses and work together, you will indeed find me. If you're not sure if you're going in the right direction, ask Kurt. He can nudge you to correct your path." Clint turned to Kurt. "Nudge."

"Fine. Fine." Kurt motioned him on. "Just get going.

Clint winked at Jody before he strolled away. He dropped his clothes in a trail behind him, knowing that Kurt would pick them up. Naked, he kept walking until he was a good half mile away from the others.

Dropping into a crouch, he called forward his wolf form.

His shift came fast. In only a few moments, he was on all fours and began to make circles. That move would tell the shifters that this was where he'd transformed. From here on out, he would be a little more careful, but he did need to give the guards a chance of finding him.

Once he'd saturated the area with his scent, Clint moved on.

Taking the most direct route, he headed straight for the compound. This would put the other shifters on alert. Their mind would begin playing tricks on them. Thinking that he was fucking with them. Not trusting their instincts. He'd told them to, but Clint knew the guards would rely on what their mind was telling them. Not what their senses were.

This was the same way that Clint learned.

To protect Sara and this town it was time to share some of his tricks.

* * * *

Sara couldn't eat another bite.

She set the last of her crust in the pizza box before sitting back and cuddling into Clint. He'd shown up in a great mood from some sort of training exercise. The pizza had been hot and greasy, which had made it perfect, and she'd even iced the beers.

With a fire roaring in front of them and a new movie playing, she was in heaven. She wanted to spend the winter nights like this. Wrapped up in Clint's arms with the threats and strangers behind them Sara wanted to enjoy the time she had with Clint. There was still one thing that she'd been hesitant about bringing up, though.

When the credits began to roll for the movie, Sara turned off the television, then turned to Clint.

"Are you staying again?" she asked. Sara asked every night and so far Clint hadn't said that he wanted to leave. Still she didn't know if she could say the words that she so badly wanted to.

"I'd like to," he replied. "Unless you want me to leave."

Sara smiled. "I never want you to leave." He could take it as a joke, but Sara finally spoke the words that had been on the tip of her tongue.

"I never want to go." He pulled her until Sara was straddling his lap.

She looked into his gaze and all the feelings she had start to bubble up. "What if you didn't have to wait for me to ask you to stay?"

"Because?"

Damn it, why was this so hard? "I know we barely know each other and you'll probably think I'm nuts but I..."

"Yes," he whispered.

"What?"

Clint chuckled nervously. "Please tell me that you're asking whether or not I want to stay here with you. Because that's all I want."

She wanted to wrap her arms around his neck and smother him with kisses. "Really?"

"Fuck, yeah."

"But what about Kurt?" She didn't want to come between the two friends. Their closeness was important and Sara liked that about them.

"Kurt is fully aware that I'm planning on being here more than at the other house. He's already told me to get on my knees and beg you to let me live here."

"Why didn't you?" It was a relief to know that he wanted to same thing and Kurt supported them.

"I didn't want to scare you away. It's true that we haven't been together long. But I've also never felt this strongly for anyone, either."

"So we're not moving too fast?" she questioned.

"I don't care if we are. This is what you want. This is what I want. If it doesn't work out, I'll join Kurt in the other place. I think it'll work out, though."

"If it doesn't it work, it won't be because we didn't give it our all," she said.

"That's right," Clint agreed.

She grasped his shoulder and leaned forward. "We're really going to do this." It wasn't a question.

"We are."

She squealed, then peppered kisses over his forehead, cheeks, then lips. Clint grabbed her face to draw her back to his mouth when she pulled away, laughing. His kiss was filled with heat, passion and promise.

Sara slipped from his lap with her lips still against his. "Let's take this somewhere more comfortable."

"Bed?"

"Our bed," she stated.

Clint picked her up, then whirled her around. She clung to him even as he carried her to the bedroom. They'd already locked up the house, but the fire was still going.

"Fire," she muttered.

"I'll get it. I have to take care of my woman first."

She was just fine with that. He laid her gently on the bed. He whipped his shirt over his head, then plucked the button of his jeans.

"I'll show you every day and night how much you mean to me. I'll make you a part of my Pack." He words were spoken like a vow.

Sara pushed herself up. "I want that. I want you to share everything with me. All of you."

"Undress for me," he said.

With her gaze locked on his, she did as he asked. They both removed their clothing. Clint's eyes were practically glowing. She'd never seen anything like it. "Wow."

"What is it?" he asked.

"You are so gorgeous," she whispered.

"Oh, no, honey. You are." He knelt on the bed between her legs. "Let me show you."

"Yes, please." Sara opened her arms and Clint moved into her embrace.

They kissed, soft and gentle. Sara ran her hands over the strong muscles of his back. Clint nibbled her bottom lip before moving down. Each brush of his lips sent a tingle through her body.

Sara wanted to feel him inside her. "Please."

Clint moved until his cock was at her entrance, the tip of his shaft piercing her.

She moaned, then scratched her nails down Clint's back. "Take me," she demanded.

He lifted his upper body off hers so he could stare down at her. Then he thrust.

Sara shouted in pleasure.

Clint grunted, growled, made every hot sound she'd ever heard.

Each time he plunged, Sara knew he was claiming her in every imaginable way. This was better than any other time. Each time they made love, she felt the connection with him deepen.

It didn't matter how long they'd been together or what had finally brought the two of them to this time and place. She and Clint belonged together.

Chapter Eleven

Clint oversaw the hand-to-hand training with a smile on his face. In just three days, the guards had been working almost nonstop. With Bobby Gibson behind bars and the town free of strangers, everyone was getting some much-needed rest. That also let them have the time to test and work with each guard.

He glanced up, spotting Kurt, Austin and Gage headed his way.

"Keep going," Clint told Ryan. He patted Ryan's shoulder, leaving the shifter in the very capable hands of RJ Cross.

"Hey, guys," Clint said after he jogged over to meet them.

"Everyone is looking good," Gage complimented.

"Thanks." Clint peered around the practice yard. "We still have some work to do, but everyone seems into the extra classes."

"I hope they stick to it," Gage said. "I'm trusting you to look after my father."

Clint turned to Kurt.

"Did I not mention that Gage's dad is one of the Alpha Council members?"

"No." Clint punched Kurt's shoulder. "You didn't."

They laughed.

"My father's the newest member of the Council, so you'll probably seeing a lot more of me. Especially if things keep going the way they are. I hate being this far from him," Gage said.

"We'll take good care of him. I promise," Kurt told him.

"He's in good hands," Clint added.

"Thanks," Gage said with a nod.

"How's Tony doing?" he asked.

"He's gone to Washington DC to meet with some government officials about Carter's group. We're hoping that we can get some help getting the Churches shut down," Austin answered.

"Colt?" Clint questioned. He knew Colt was a part of Austin's Pack.

"Still under." Austin sighed. "I didn't realize when I gave Colt permission to do this mission it would end up taking so long. I can see the toll it's taking on him."

"Remember we're here to help," Clint said. "If you need any help, just let us know."

"We will," Austin agreed.

"Maybe you'll make it down to Texas to see me and my mate. Bring your girl," Gage said.

Clint grinned. He liked Sara being described as his.

"Speaking of Sara," Kurt said. "The guard house just called. She was at the gate. I had them direct her here."

"What?"

Kurt laughed. "I think she's pulling up now."

Clint whirled around. Sure enough, Sara was pulling up to a small paved parking area set to the side of where they were training. He was already jogging over by the time he heard his friend's laughter. Clint just ignored them. Why was Sara there? Was something wrong? And Cecil was with her. Did this have something to do with Ryan?

"Hey," she said after she'd climbed out of her car.

"Are you okay?" Clint asked. He ran his gaze over her, but Sara was smiling and didn't appear injured. Cecil walked up beside them as he waved to Ryan.

"Fine," she said. "You?"

"Good, good." He was confused. Clint shifted on his feet, nerves biting at him. He needed Sara and his Pack to like each other. She'd just never been around this many shifters. He didn't want her scared. Not that she appeared to be. She was glancing around with interest.

"I'm dropping Cecil off. Ryan is taking him away for the weekend," Sara said. She had a smile on her face. "Ryan asked if I wouldn't mind bringing him so they can leave from here. I hope that's okay."

"I was hoping to catch some of his training," Cecil whispered. "He's been working on his moves at my place and it's so hot."

"Oh." Clint chuckled. "Well, I think we can arrange something." He motioned for them both to follow.

"We have an audience," RJ told Ryan. "I guess I should go easy on you in front of your boyfriend." The taunt did its job. Ryan growled before crouching low.

"Hell no," Ryan replied. "My man already knows what a badass I am. It's a good thing your mates not here to see me take you done."

"Oh!" RJ jumped around as he grinned.

Clint swung his arm around Sara's shoulder. "This is going to be great."

Her nose was wrinkled as she glanced at him. The confusion just made her so damn cute. "What?"

"We call RJ our little puppy dog," Clint said. "He's like the biggest kid ever. This is going to be fun."

"He's not going to hurt Ryan is he?" Sara frowned then looked over to where Cecil was standing to get a better view.

"Of course not," Clint assured her. "This is actually a good look at the Pack."

"What do you mean?"

"RJ will joke and tease Ryan which will get him comfortable. RJ is also one of the most highly trained fighters I've ever met. But the way he teaches has the younger shifters not realizing they're learning until they complete the move. A lot of how we fight in instinct and RJ shows them that. Plus with Cecil here I'm certain that RJ will concentrate on what Ryan excells at."

"So this is for fun?" she asked.

"Fun and good training," Clint corrected. "If there ever comes a time that Ryan has to defend Cecil they'll both know that Ryan can take care of him."

Sara leaned into his side. "So it's like an older brother teaching someone to defend themselves?"

"Exactly."

She tugged at her shirt. "Thanks for letting me watch. I was worried that you wouldn't want me here."

Clint didn't like that at all. He moved to stand in front of her. "Why would you think that? Is it something I've said? Done?"

"No," she said quickly. When she looked away Clint knew something was bothering her.

He grasped her elbow gently to tug her away from the crowd. Cecil and the shifters were gathering around Ryan and RJ as they started. "Talk to me," he pleaded. "Tell me what's wrong."

"Nothing's wrong." She flushed. "This is stupid. Let's just watch Ryan."

Clint caught her hand and brought her palm up his mouth. He loved touching her, didn't think he'd ever tire of having his hands on her. But it was her scent that really drove him crazy. Sometime without him noticing their scent had combined on almost everything he owned. His clothes, his belongings, even him. "There's something going on in that head of yours."

"Do you-" She blew out a breath. Then laughed. "Shit."

"Do I what?" he pressed.

"Would you prefer if I was a shifter?" she asked. Her voice was so quiet that even with his enhanced hearing he almost missed her question.

"I can't-" He pulled her further away from everyone. To the end of the training field. No one should be able to hear them from this far back. "I have never wished you were shifter instead of human."

"So you've always preferred human woman?" She nodded. Although there were lines netween her eyes showing her confusion.

"Where is this coming from?" he demanded. If someone was trying scare her away he'd kill them.

"There was a program last night that said-"

He barked out a laugh. "Stop. Stop right there."

She looked at him.

"Whatever you were watching was probably some kind of screwed up human program," he told her. "It doesn't matter if you're a shifter or human. It was you that I fell in love with. You. From how you take care of Cecil, your dad, and this entire town. It's because of who you are that I want to be with you. Not what you are."

Before he even finished speaking she was nodding. "So I'm being stupid?"

"No," he assured her. "It's a smart question. And we should make sure that there are no misunderstandings between us."

"Okay, sorry. I don't even know why I started to worry about it."

Clint shook his head. "There's nothing for you to be sorry about."

"I think we missed the fight," she pointed toward the field.

He glanced over his shoulder at the guards who had been training. Apparently, the session was over. Ryan and several of the others were laughing and joking while making their way up to the main building. "Well, I have a better idea anyway — how about a tour?"

"Really?" Sara bounced. "Is that allowed?"

"Sure." He was living with Sara now, she was a part of his life. Hell, he'd committed to her being Pack. It was time to join his two worlds together. "Come on."

She slipped her hand in his and he tugged her behind him. He had so much that he wanted to show her. This land spoke to him and he was very interested to see how she reacted.

"Where are we going?" she asked.

"I want to show you my favorite spot," he said.

"Cool!" She followed along, but swung her gaze this way and that so she could take in the scenery. "It's so pretty here."

"This land has seen some tough times, but the stronger the Pack, the more it flourishes. It's our job to make sure the territory is here for the next generations," he said. Clint had lowered his voice, which just felt right as they stepped between two giant oaks.

"You're taking me into the forest to savage me, right?"

He glanced over his shoulder and winked. "You scared?"

Sara pushed his shoulder. "Not even a little bit."

"Good." Clint pointed toward the trail off to the side. "If you ever come out here alone, you need to follow the path. If you get lost out here, it could take hours to find you."

"But we're not going that way, though."

"Well, no," he said. "I don't have to follow the rules."

"Oh!" she drawled. "A rebel."

"No," he corrected. "I know every inch of this land. I've spent hours and hours in my wolf form in the woods."

"I'd like to see that again," she said. "I love both your forms."

Clint turned before he drew her closer. "Both, huh?"

"Well, there are times that I am more partial to your hard, sexy body." She ran her hands over his chest. He'd only pulled on a muscle tank earlier since his schedule had put him training all morning. "But I don't mind petting a very pretty fur coat, either."

"Pretty?" Clint lifted a brow. He was not pretty.

Sara grinned. "Handsome?"

"That's better."

"Unbelievable."

"A lot better." He gripped her hips and yanked her forward. There was no way she wouldn't feel his erection. Every time she touched him, he got hard. "Now, stop distracting me. I want you to see my spot. It'll give us more privacy."

He pulled a laughing Sara behind him.

Clint might be the hunter, but it was Sara who had caught him.

The welcoming smile she'd always had for him. Not judging him for being a shifter. Yeah, his life had been good up to this point, but with Sara, he was complete. No matter what happened from here on out, she'd be at his side. And that made him so fucking happy.

Want to see more from this author? Here's a taster for you to enjoy!

Bear Claw
Crissy Smith

Excerpt

Jamie Ward pulled his Harley up in front of the Lake Worth Public Library and parked in the first space. It was rare for him to have a full weekend off, but he'd managed to get both Saturday and Sunday free.

After spending the day catching up on house chores and shopping, he was now prepared to spend his Sunday the way he wanted.

First up was hitting the place for some new books. He could have gone to one of the three major book retailers but he much preferred atmosphere of the old building and the helpful employees.

Plus the library actually had a better selection. More diverse anyway. Instead of stocking up on only the bestsellers, like the chain stores, here a little bit of everything was available. It was interesting to him that such a small, county-funded business would be able to provide him with anything he wanted.

After he'd moved to Lake Worth from Phoenix, he'd taken his bike around to check out his new neighborhood. He'd spotted the old, worn brick building and had felt the strong urge to go inside.

One visit had turned into two then three, and now he was a regular patron.

Jamie swung his leg off the bike and stood, stretching. Even though it was officially the end of summer, the heat was still stifling at ten in the morning.

As he reached the entrance, a young woman exited the structure with a small male child. It didn't surprise him that she steered the youngster as far away from him as possible.

As a big guy, Jamie's size was enough to make most people apprehensive of him, but add in his numerous tats and piercings, and he literally scared people.

He hadn't been going after that reaction when he'd first started his markings. Well, that wasn't completely honest. His appearance did a lot to help keep criminals in their place. Since he'd accepted his new position at the Shifter Coalition as the leader of the Black Bear Division, he'd used his looks several times to intimidate suspects.

He was proud of his body art. However, he didn't want others to feel uncomfortable. So he hung back, stuffing his hands in his jeans, letting the woman and child pass without trouble. After they'd reached the stairs, he moved into the dark, cool entry.

Arriving so early on a Sunday, he knew he wouldn't have to deal with too many other people. He liked this time of day. He could browse to his heart's content and see what great new finds he could pick up.

Since he knew the entire layout by memory, Jamie first headed to the new release section. He leafed through the shelf, picking up and disregarding one book after another until he settled on the latest thriller from a popular author.

Jamie enjoyed reading the writer's work, even if the middle of his books were rather dull. The beginning and ending of each story always made up for the boring chapters.

Tucking the hardback under his arm, he turned and almost collided into one of the rolling carts.

"Sorry," the woman pushing exclaimed. "I didn't think you were done yet."

Jamie looked up and grinned. And there was the other reason he chose the library instead of the city bookstores.

Most of the staff had gotten used to him and all were friendly enough but the woman in front of him was by far his favourite employee.

She'd welcomed him on his first visit then had shown him around. Jamie always made a habit of stopping by whatever section she was stocking and talking to her for a few minutes.

"Brandy," he said cheerfully. "How are you?"

A smile bloomed across her face. "I'm great. Yesterday was hectic, so there are more books to put back than normal, but it was a fun day. Well worth the extra work now."

Jamie shifted a little closer. Even though Brandy had been kind and open, Jamie always tried to keep his distance. She might not seem intimidated by him but he didn't know for sure. He would have flirted with her on more than one occasion except he was certain he wasn't her type.

A pretty and smart girl, Brandy could do a lot better than the likes of him. Still, he would enjoy her company every chance he got.

Had she moved closer to him, or was it his imagination? Giving himself a minute to gather his composure, he glanced around the small section where they stood. His gaze fell on the poster of children sitting around in a reading circle.

Brandy's project! He wanted to smack himself. "So the reading went well?" Jamie had forgotten that on Saturdays the library had started a children's reading program.

Brandy had been so excited about it and it was all she'd talked about on his last few visits. If he had remembered, he would have stopped by and shown his support.

"Yes! We had fifteen kids show up and all of them ended up checking out at least one book. All the parents enjoyed the break and said they would be back for the next one," she said.

"That's awesome. All your hard work really paid off."

She blushed, which was as cute as anything he had ever seen. "Your suggestions on where to hang the notices around the neighbourhood really helped. Over half of the adults told us they had seen the flyers."

"That's good." Jamie was glad his suggestions had worked. Since he constantly watched his surroundings, he'd noticed where children seemed to hang out. "I'm glad."

"It's so important that kids get the chance to visit. Most of the parents in the area can't afford the high prices at the chain stores and now they know they can come here for free."

Brandy was practically bouncing on the balls of her feet with happiness. Jamie's heart swelled. In his world, he saw so much ugliness. Brandy was a breath of fresh air to a hardened man like himself.

"I wish you could have seen how excited everyone was."

Jamie made a mental note to drop by the next reading circle, no matter what. He'd have to stay back to make sure he didn't upset the kids or their parents, but he wanted to see Brandy in her element. "Me too."

"So enough about that. What are you looking for today?"

Jamie held up the book he'd chosen. "I was just browsing. I'm about to head over to the north section. I looked up some books on spirituality and I wanted to see if you had any in stock."

"Oh, cool." Brandy shoved the overflowing cart of books to the side and motioned for him to follow her. "Actually, we have several new titles that I've put out in the last couple of weeks. And I think there is one that you have to read. I finished it in one night. I couldn't put it down."

Jamie followed her through the long rows of bookcases, listening to her speak in quiet but animated tones. It didn't matter who the author was or whether he was interested in the book, he would check it out to keep that brightness in her eyes.

Rounding a corner, Brandy paused to let another patron pass and Jamie didn't miss the onceover the guy gave her. She didn't notice the other man's attention. Brandy smiled politely, still talking to Jamie, and he had to work to keep the smirk off his face.

About the Author

Crissy Smith lives in Texas with her husband, daughter, and three Labrador retrievers. The three dogs love to curl up under her computer desk and nap while she writes. It doesn't leave a lot of room for her but what's a woman to do?

When not writing or reading, she enjoys hunting, camping and shooting. But she has a girly side too and is addicted to pedicures and coffee.

She has been writing since she was a teenager and still loves everything to do with the paranormal. Her stories and characters all have a place in her heart. She loves the Alpha male, the dominant werewolf, and the Master vampire, which find their way in most of her books.

Learn more about the characters she has created at her website where they have their very own page. It will be updated from time to time to let you know what's going on with them. Also you can find out who will be in the next book.

Crissy loves to hear from readers. You can find her contact information, website details and author profile page at http://www.totallybound.com.

Home of Erotic Romance